THE TELENKOVIAN EXPERIMENT

M. J. Politis

Ph.D., D.V.M., H.B.AR.P.

276 5th Avenue Suite 704 #944

New York, NY 10001

Copyright © 2025 M. J. Politis

ISBN (Paperback) 978-1-80704-258-5

ISBN (Hardback) 978-1-80704-259-2

ISBN (eBook) 978-1-80704-257-8

Cover Design by Woodbridge Publishers.

Find out more about our upcoming releases and authors at www.woodbridgepublishers.com and sign up for our newsletter to stay updated!

CHAPTER 1

Senior pilot Johnny "I.B." Good boldly spoke into the intercom with a proud New Orleans drawl. "We will be landing in Leningrad soon. Please see that your papers are in order and that your seat belts are securely fastened."

"Why should I have my papers in order in a country where everything is in chaos?" L. Geoffrey Weinburg said to himself. He had earned his Ph.D. at the age of 25 and snatched a full professor post at Harvard Medical School by his thirtieth birthday. The track up to Chairman, Dean, then Associate High Priest was written in cyberspace and stone. The big Four-O and mid-life crisis were a lifetime away, reserved for the schleps who still had to sweat their way to the top.

Geoff wouldn't listen to anyone and was well paid for being colorfully arrogant. "Cool," some called it. He didn't have to obey the rules that average people had to live by.

Still, Geoff buckled up, knowing full well that cutting-edge American-made landing gear could still be challenged by the Soviet-built concrete strip, which had more potholes than the West Side Highway during a construction strike.

As the wheels hit the ground, Geoff's stomach churned. Perhaps it was jet lag, or maybe because he was alone this time. Wife, mistress, and female graduate students were all half a world away. His Russian hosts requested no more than two people from his lab, the soon-to-be-ex-Soviet authorities allowing only one visa to be granted.

Still, it was an adventure. And a time to meet Yakov again. Geoff and Yakov went through graduate school together at "the Rock," the ultimate biomedical endurance test of egos and sometimes character. Rockefeller University grads were the best in the world. Who else would be called in to examine a patient who provided a key to understanding Soviet Russia's past and post-Soviet Russia's future?

The confidential documents Geoff got in the mail hinted at something big about this one. "An epidemic that could be bigger than AIDS," the report projected, using colored bar graphs to make its point more vividly visual.

It could be true, Geoff thought in the recesses of his mind. And it was "Top Secret." But that term was never taken seriously by Ivy League tower geniuses. Geoff remembered how Susan Mautone "confidentially" told him in the early eighties that fifteen percent of the blood samples from West Point Cadets tested HIV positive. Whether it was true or not didn't matter. She was trapped by student loans, a bad academic average, and child support payments. Susan desperately tried to avoid death by boredom. And she missed no opportunity to share a secret, particularly if it could sexually arouse someone who could rescue her from a lifetime of cleaning test tubes and changing diapers.

But in 1982, Geoff's concerns were on getting himself into a top-flight post-doc program, and he could smell trailer park ugly beneath Susan's supermodel body. Besides, the fate of a few thousand or a million military grunts never entered into Geoff's mind. The always-on-the-cutting-edge rising star of the biochemistry department was interested in molecules, not epidemics.

In the nineties, Geoff's skepticism of epidemic rumors was based in reality, particularly in the Soviet Union. No one, even the Russian academics, believed half of what was printed in the Soviet scientific journals. After all, this was a country that documented the highest number of ET landing sites in the world. Rumors of demons had driven terror into millions of Russian serfs before the Bolshevik Revolution, and propaganda allowed unspeakable acts of terror to continue unchecked after the 1917 liberation. Misinformation was the way the Soviet Union conducted all its business, even in these new Glasnost times. "Secretly" bringing Geoff over to the Soviet Union on a medical fact-finding tour on a new epidemic was smart politics. What better way for the bureaucrats at the Communicable Disease Agency in Atlanta, the Ministry of Science in Moscow, and an "unnamed" pharmaceutical company to get World Health Organization funding? The trick had been pulled off before, and Geoff would play his part, as cast.

Geoff imagined Russian customs to be like an Orwellian black and white late-night re-run. It was a lot more colorful than that.

The faded pictures of Bolshevik heroes were blurred in the memory of the customs inspectors who were more worried about biological survival than political ideology. With freedom came liberation, but also uncertainty. The unwritten rules were more complicated now, and particularly harsh for those who still needed rules.

Janitors at the Moscow McDonald's were paid more than neurosurgeons, and mobsters were paid better than anybody. The lifetime gratitude of a Medical Institute Director or a Cabinet Minister could be obtained with a canned ham. A roll of Kodak film cost $5, a week's wage. A 120-proof bottle of vodka cost less than a dime and was drunk to excess by beggar and banker alike.

"Where do you live?" the customs inspector asked with a civil and even tone.

Manhattan in the winter. Montauk during the summer," Geoff answered.

A look of forgiving disapproval, then another question. "What does the 'L' in your name stand for, Doctor Weinburg?"

"Nothing I'd repeat in mixed company," Geoff replied.

From the officer, a look of puzzlement. Then determination.

"Lorie," Geoff said quietly, remembering the painful days of his childhood before gender-neutral names were acceptable in the boys' locker room.

The officer smiled, silently enjoying his final say in the cultural joust.

At the end of the hallway, a five-foot-ten supermodel with platinum hair down to her waist. She looked like she belonged in Malibu, not Leningrad. On the sign around her neck, "MISTER Weinburg." Behind it, some medical anatomy that Geoff would be very interested in examining.

She didn't speak. Just smiled. All the way to the airport exit. There, in a BMW rebuilt with VW and Ford parts - Yakov.

"Geoff, good to see you...."

Yakov's handshake was firm, his eyes vibrant. Geoff's hair had gotten shorter over the years. Yakov's was longer, and a beard added to complement it. Around his neck, a choker, perhaps Cherokee, maybe Siberian.

"How are things?" Yakov asked.

"Good, good," Geoff replied. "You look good. Good."

"You look good, too. Good to see you."

They exchanged stories about the past, some rehearsed and some re-composed on the spot.

It was a long ride to the Korinska Institute. Geoff talked about how the American empire would crumble soon after it devoured what was left of the crumbling Soviet empire, and how the Malaysians would make a windfall killing after everyone went bankrupt. "But, one day, the rats and cockroaches will take it all back again. The most intelligent and underestimated creatures on the fucking planet," he concluded.

Yakov smiled. "Rats in Moscow were even bigger than in New York, and twice as bold." He sighed, then put an envelope in Geoff's lap, labeled "Top Secret." Yakov added his own qualifier - "FOR REAL," and he meant it. "Geoff, YOUR government said that WE have a communicable health problem. The truth is that we ALL have a GLOBAL EPIDEMIC, God help us."

Yakov never used the word "God," except when trying to go one-up on a Woody Allen one-liner. Geoff read the contents of the envelope, slowly and carefully. It contained a photograph and some lab work. Some of the data was within normal range. Most of it was too far off the scale to be anything except laboratory error, he thought.

"Yakov, the name here is Sergei. An ex-farmer. Ninety years old. I thought that our index case was patient number 123,556. Named Nicholi. A construction worker."

"He uses a lot of names. Claims to be many ages. Sometimes he's an old man, sometimes a young woman. It's like he became a whole group of people. Like ghosts of

a whole community of dead people take turns using his body."

Yakov was direct, cold, and scared. The remote research institution they drove into didn't make Geoff feel any easier. The imported security gates were originally designed by Texas Instruments to keep Russian spies out of the Niki missile bases. The guards were top-notch professionals, the best six-figure mercenaries the Russian government could buy, and the most loyal military soldiers they could find. No Rambo wannabes or Afghanistan burn-outs.

The interview room could have been anywhere in the upscale industrialized world, generically comfortable and impersonal. A wooden table, three chairs, a coffee mug, and railings along the side with notches that could hold coffee, chairs, and restraints, as required. The noise was "white," like the walls.

An old man was brought in, mumbling in Ukrainian. His body could be blown over by a breeze from an open window, but his eyes were bright blue and blazed with the fire of passion. He looked angrily at Yakov, then inquisitively at Geoff.

"Boris," Yakov said. "My friend wants to hear your story. Tell him your story."

The old man asked for a cigarette. He coughed, blood spewing from his mouth, his limbs shivering in the 90-degree mid-summer heat.

Yakov reached into his pocket, retrieving a pack of Camels, unfiltered and unopened, the only brand the old man liked and trusted.

"He needs oxygen, not a fucking cigarette," Geoff said in his usual understated authoritative tone.

Yakov gave Boris a cigarette. "His body doesn't obey the rules anymore."

The Ukrainian asked Geoff for a light with a piercing stare. Yakov pulled out a tin match box, gold plated with a skillfully crafted relief of a Roman interspecies orgy. He put it on the table. As Boris reached out, Geoff pulled it away, but not before the old man had snatched a match.

Boris struck a match on one of his three remaining teeth and lit up. He took a slow, deliberate draw, holding it in long enough for the smoke to penetrate into his gnarly fingers. With a second drag, he grabbed the match box from Geoff's clammy fingers and crushed the tin box into bits, smiling as he let the metallic dust fall into a thirty-cent plastic ashtray.

"Vodka," Boris demanded.

The Orderly accommodated his request. The door was locked, and the security system was on full alert. Boris nodded. Yakov turned on the tape recorder. The story began to flow through the old Ukrainian's six-inch mustache, his hauntingly clear diction unimpeded by a mouthful of missing teeth and partial paralysis of his left jaw. Yakov translated. Geoff listened.

Reel 1

Tasha used all the strength of her frail, ninety-eight-pound body to carry a crate of hand-painted dishes into the community hall, a weather-beaten barn we once called the church. She was wearing her Grandmother's Easter dress, three sizes too big this year, two sizes too small last season. She looked up at the blue sky through the hole in the roof, then knelt, then crossed herself at the wooden crucifix carved into the North Wall. She slowly rose, then set the table for the most important dinner the village of Telenkov would share in the winter of 1932.

The table was a workbench, and the floor belonged to the field mice and the rats as much as us. It was unusual for us to share dinners on special occasions with anyone except family. But it was a special occasion and, whether we wanted it or not, we were all part of one family in Telenkov in that year.

Tasha's soul never seemed right for her body. She always felt that her breasts were too big or her hands were not big enough. She never let her long, black hair flow down her back in public, and never in the company of men. She was always concerned about appearances, even in the worst of times. The real reasons were reserved for herself and her Creator.

Tasha insisted on setting out the dishes and candlesticks that somehow survived three Czars, a World War, the Korinski uprising of Spring, 1917, the Bolshevik revolution of Fall, 1917, and a civil war that lingered on in the Ukraine till the Fall of '22, even though they tell me the history books say it ended in '20.

It was late March. The air had started to thaw in February, a gift from a South wind that had caressed the Steppes, after a cold snap that had lasted since before Christmas. But the ground was still hard as a rock, and the green of Springtime was still frozen in our frostbitten imaginations. As was Nicholi's skill with a hammer and nails.

"I'll fix the roof right this time. I went to school to be a carpenter, and I'll be damned to hell if winter will beat me again," he said, as he repaired the roof for the third time that week. Most anyone walking on two legs, and a few creatures who walked on four, could have done a better job than Nicholi. But Nicholi was the village carpenter, and even if we didn't respect his position, we admired his persistence. He was born to the woods, with a growl of a bear, the front teeth of a badger, and a mustache thicker than Stalin's, a fact in which he took much pride. No one was more determined to convert rotted wood and rusted metal into shelter. Still, we flinched with pain and shivered with cold as he continued to hammer as many nails through his palms as into the roof.

Of course, someone had to argue. This time it was Johan. "We could be using that lumber for firewood." He was six-foot-five, clean-shaven even on the coldest winter days, and as overweight as anyone could get in Telenkov. He naturally appointed himself Mayor. No one else really wanted the job. The Polish-French businessman found his way into Ukraine after the 1917 revolution, and then wouldn't, or couldn't, leave. He never told us why.

Johan didn't talk much, but he screamed a lot. He didn't really understand that in Telenkov, we expected people of the lowest character to be in the highest political positions. Maybe that was why we always had rotten rulers.

Maybe it was just something about being Ukrainian or, as we were supposed to now call ourselves, "Soviet."

"The wood you wasted trying to fix these roofs could heat ten houses for a week. That's two hundred and thirty thousand kilocalories of heat. Do you know how much heat is in two hundred and thirty thousand kilocalories?" Johan continued. He tried to convince us with more mathematics, a lingering effect of the days when he was an investment banker. But no one in Telenkov cared about banking or understood much mathematics.

"The horses," Sergei grumbled. There wasn't an inch of skin on Sergei that wasn't covered by hair, except on his head, which he always kept covered, even in private, so I was told. "We could have used the horses for meat this year. They were getting old and had no more than one or two more winters left in them, anyway. If I get my hands on whoever stole them, I'll kill him."

Elena looked down. As Sergei's wife, she had to do what he commanded, especially in public. What she did at the corral gate a few months earlier was brave and smart. Elena was one of the most beautiful women in Telenkov, but she always thought she was the ugliest. Her eyes were big, making her face look small, but her soul was bigger than life.

Elena hoped that the hay and winter grass in the bluffs would be enough to sustain the village horses, and that the animals would have enough sense to hide from people until cold weather and hot tempers blew over.

Elena told only her two most trusted friends about the hiding place she found for the horses, the faithful beasts who even the always-angry Sergei loved more than any other people in the village. But, like vitality, poverty, and character, secrets were valued in Telenkov and well-kept. Or so Elena hoped, as the supply trucks from Moscow continued to come through the Ukraine empty, and return overloaded with supplies.

We were told that it was an emergency situation. That Comrade Stalin needed all the food the Ukraine could produce to build a Socialist Paradise. Comrade Stalin was not someone to be argued with. We feared him more than any other Russian, maybe because his roots were not Russian, a public fact we were not supposed to know. We were more frightened about what had happened to us, and why God had allowed us to keep living in a winter when there was so much dying everywhere else. Perhaps a special torture awaited us at the hands of Stalin on earth, and the devil in hell. But some of us, like Anna, always knew that it was better to do, rather than to be done to. And we all had to be ready for the guest who was coming.

Our guest was, in title, the Bolshevik officer in charge of our village. In reality, he was a mirror that reflected our souls. His fate, and ours, would depend on how dignified we could appear, and how courageous we could be.

Anna folded up fragments of what used to be silk Parisian undergarments into napkins, placing them under the polished forks and spoons. Tasha was not happy about her family treasures being window-dressed by someone with Anna's reputation and unofficially recognized profession. But Tasha realized that Anna knew when to provide for a man's needs, and when not to satisfy his desires. Tasha also realized that if we fought each other, the only winners would be the Soviet authorities and the Ukrainian winter. Besides, Anna was part of the communal effort to keep Telenkov alive, whether we, or she, liked it or not.

No one knew where Anna had come from, or whether she was motivated by lust, love, or a will to survive. Maybe it was all three at once.

More mumbling built up into more arguing. It was always the same, even in the "good" seasons after 1922.

We would complain about too much rain, or too little rain, often at the same time. We complained, worried, and argued with God, something the atheists were very good at. But some of us just kept working.

By the time the table was set, Nicholi had patched up the roof, the way HE wanted it fixed, ignoring how many kilocalories of heat he wasted. The lumber belonged to him more than anyone else, anyway. It was scrap wood, taken from what was left of the Soviet Army wagons that had been stranded in the village. A very large number of wagons mysteriously broke a spoke or an axle when they came into Telenkov, and Nicholi was very skillful in making fixable wagons look unfixable to suspicious Bolshevik officers.

The duty-bound soldiers who volunteered to remain behind waiting for repairs rarely returned home to Moscow, Kiev, or Leningrad. If they did, they brought back no news about what was really going on behind closed doors and downward-looking eyes in Telenkov.

Telenkov was one of the most popular unknown villages in Ukraine. What really happened that winter could only be understood from the heart. From a Telenkovian heart. You see, we were a simple people. A practical people. And tied to the ways of the land. Or maybe we weren't...

Easter came early that year. We weren't supposed to be Christians, now that we were liberated from our bondage to the Church. To the militant Soviets, it was my birthday we were celebrating. To the more intellectual Bolsheviks, we were celebrating a Festival Day from "pagan" times, when the Ukraine honored God and the Earth at the same time, something that we still did, despite Father Dimitri's threats about going to hell with the other pagans, a term which included Jews, Moslems, and sometimes Roman Catholics. His long hair and beard made Father Dimitri look like a Saint, and when you obeyed the commandments he passed down. His bloodshot eyes threw fire at you when you defied his authority. Father Dimitri's power over us came from two sources. He was one of the only people in our village who could read, and the only one who claimed to have God's mandate behind each of his opinions.

What we believed about any Deity didn't matter anyway, especially then. We came to Church to pray with each other, not to God. You came with an open heart, a dedication to better yourself in the future, and a set of cotton balls inside your ears so that the painful off-tune singing of the person next to you didn't drive you insane.

Finally, the table was set and all the decorations were in place. According to tradition, the wind whisked the consciousness of those who had faith into the realm of the Spirits, and those who did not have faith into the world of imagination.

Visiting our feast were the ghosts of many uninvited, and unanticipated, Spirits. We still had meat on our ribs, a situation which was not so in the other Ukrainian communities, which had been starved to death by February. Why were we allowed to survive when so many others died? Were we blessed by God, or did we make a deal with the Devil to save our bodies, losing our souls in the process?

Finally, someone mentioned the one word that was on our minds. "Major Rusmonski." It was Elena who had the courage to break the silence this time. "Will he be with us today?"

All eyes turned to me. It was my job to deal with the District Commander. We had an election and took a vote. It was a split, half for and half against. As the town worrier, and the person who knew the Major best, it was left to me.

"Well, is he going to be here or not?" Johan asked, his authoritative eyes showing a fear that he had never revealed in public before.

There was a knock on the door. I knew it would be coming, and that things between us and the Major would never be the same again once we encountered who, or what, was on the other side. It was Judgment Day on Earth for ALL of us.

I found myself remembering how things came to this, hoping to understand why, so I could prepare myself for the fate which I had inflicted on the only real friends I ever had.

CHAPTER 2

The cigarette was finished. Boris, as he preferred to call himself that day, was silent. Reflective. Remorseful. But still undefeated.

Geoff could never get used to seeing defiance in the eyes of old people. It scared him. It also reminded him of his Uncle Sol, the closest thing Geoff had to a father. Solomon Weinburg was a self-taught immigrant electrician who could barely read a manual. But he could read a panel circuit with the tips of his fingers, and became more skilled in the ways of American business than any fifth-generation Yankee blue blood. It was a tragedy that Parkinson's disease converted his hands into shaking leaves. His last year was marked by more internal tragedy and regret in his heart, for unfulfilled dreams and the inability to correct past wrongs done to innocent people in more optimistic times.

Young Geoffrey visited his Uncle Sol every Saturday, his young eyes on the floor or his watch. There was something about old age that terrified Geoff, even as a fourteen-year-old. Maybe it was the loss of dignity. Maybe it was the accountability of it all.

Yakov gave Boris another cigarette and lit it with one of the matches that had fallen on the floor.

"How much more do you want to hear?" Boris asked in his native language, the only one he spoke in public. Though fluent in Yakov's language, Boris refused to speak it. Speaking Russian would burn his tongue, an old Ukrainian wives' tale that the old man chose to believe in the winter years of a life that had gone on too long already.

Geoff was bored and made no attempt to hide it. "Yakov. I came here to look at an index case for a communicable psychiatric disease. Not to listen to an old man's ghost stories."

"There are no ghost stories," Boris answered - in English.

Once again, the penetrating stare. Boris would not tolerate a greedy American Capitalist insulting his dignity. The old geezer had many showdowns with Muscovite Yuppies. All lived to regret the day they gave that "I was born better than you" look to the crazy Ukrainian gunslinger.

But Geoff still valued sophistication above grit. "Yakov. What does this ghost story have to do with an epidemic which YOU claim has killed thousands, and which will kill millions if we don't stop it?"

"Everything, 'Lorie'," Boris replied. No one except the FBI and a few relatives biding their time in Long Island nursing homes knew what the mysterious "L" stood for in Geoff's name, not even Yakov.

The eminent Doctor Weinburg was beyond baffled. Though he claimed to hate boredom above all things, Geoff was terrified of not knowing exactly what would happen next.

The old man lit up another cigarette. Very smooth. Very satisfied.

"He knows a lot more than we give him credit for," Yakov said. "A lot more than he gives himself credit for."

Boris smiled warmly this time. He talked a little louder. Geoff listened a little harder.

Reel 2

We were always ignored by the world. Everything came late to us, or not at all. Even the collective farms. We didn't have enough people or farmable land to make it worth the Soviets putting us on the payroll of "volunteer" workers, in the agricultural Paradise that was going to feed the USSR for a thousand years, until 1932. Telenkov was barely on the UKRAINIAN maps. We were one of the best-kept secrets in Ukraine, from ourselves and the world. Still, the Bolsheviks would never let any corner of their empire remain the same. There was a principle at stake for them.

The changes started for us in September. Or maybe it was October. The harvest was good, very good. Nadia said it was too good, but nobody listened to Nadia much. For everything bad that happened, she said it was because something good was to come soon, and for every good thing that happened, God would make us suffer. "That which didn't kill us would make us more Ukrainian," was the joke going around. It was not original, but then again, nothing in Telenkov was.

Nadia worried more than even I did. She worried about the living and the dead. Whenever anyone died, they were sure to get three things in Telenkov. A flood of tears from the mourners, a droning eulogy from Father Dimitri, and garlic cloves on the grave for three days from Nadia, so the vampires didn't trap the soul inside the body before it was ready to ascend to heaven.

Nadia watched the sky a lot, especially in the fall. She could see a cold winter coming through the third eye above her four-inch hooked nose. A small cloud of smoke hovered over the horizon, merely a burst of dust against a clear blue sky to the eye, not used to inner vision on the high plains.

"The horses," Nadia warned Elena as they harvested the last of the fall wheat, tips so heavy with seed that they bent the stalks nearly to the ground. "You have to hide the horses."

"Why?" Elena asked. Nobody asked Nadia "why" very much, maybe because her answers would only confuse you even more. But this time she answered, clearly and distinctly.

"We have to have something left in the Spring that we value. People with nothing left to value are not people anymore. They are worse than dead." Nadia's response was brief and firm. "I have to warn the other villages, even though it is already too late. You must stay here. For the sake of your children. Promise me that you will hide the horses."

Elena was baffled. Though a mother to three children by the age of twenty, Elena was still only a girl in many ways. She obeyed people with determined eyes, and Nadia's eyes were more determined than ever.

By sunrise of the next day, the half-Jewish sorceress, whom we Christians revered in bad times and laughed at in good times, was gone. In her place, a convoy of Russian trucks and tanks. We had never seen so many trucks and tanks. Then there were the boots. Leather boots, on even the most lowly privates. Shiny boots with wooden heels. The best we had were hides to cover our feet, rags when times were not so good. We envied those boots, and the Russians knew it. We felt inferior, like lower-class people. It was the Russians' most powerful weapon, and they never failed to use it against us.

A Colonel in a freshly pressed uniform came out of his car. Colonels never came to Telenkov. The only thing we had in abundant in Telenkov was boredom. And, of course, wheat.

Johan stood up. As Mayor, he loved to make jokes in public. "Kiev is three hundred kilometers east, Colonel. You must have gotten lost. No one of any importance comes to Telenkov unless it's by accident, or bad luck." Johan needed to think he was funny, so we laughed. It was a Ukrainian joke, not really understandable to a Russian.

The Colonel smiled. Maybe he was part Ukrainian. He lifted his finger. The soldiers opened fire.

The gunshots echoed through our ears, piercing into our shattered minds. Then the boot heels stomped through the streets, kicking in the doors of every house. Before we could find the ground with our feet, we were in the village square, surrounded by soldiers with visors covering their eyes.

We watched. Watched them take away any food they could carry. Watched them take away any weapons we could use against them. Watched them leave us stranded against the oncoming winter.

"Comrades," the Russian Colonel said sarcastically, knowing fully well that we remained as neutral as we could when the Reds and Whites were using the Ukraine as a battleground in 1919. "The revolution needs food. Next time, we will come back for more food, or for some of you."

With that, the Colonel nodded his finger, and the waves of soldiers left. We were lucky, I suppose. As soon as they were out of range of our voices, Nicholi spoke. "The Russians will be back to take everything else we have, too. They take away your dignity slowly, so it hurts more."

Nicholi always overreacted to the Russians, but he was entitled to. He had signed on with the Volunteer White Brigade in December 1919 and wound up a POW in January 1920. The exploits about how he escaped - and found his way home - were legend in Telenkov. What he experienced behind the barbed wire fences was always a mystery.

The next visit, the soldiers raided the cellars. It was the first place we could think of to hide whatever spare or rotted food we could find, so naturally it was the first place the Russians looked. They prided themselves on outsmarting us.

When they took what we needed to keep our bodies alive, they came for what we used to keep our souls from dying. "Gold should be used in the service of your fellow Comrades, not a bourgeois God who keeps the masses oppressed by Imperial Capitalists," the Colonel said, as they stole the icons and crucifixes from the Church, leaving behind a pile of ashes and a stack of Communist Manifestos. It would only be a matter of time till they came for the gold fillings in our teeth.

It all happened so quickly. The destruction.. The disorientation. The hunger. And the dying, for those lucky enough to be old and sick. Stories were reaching us about entire villages disappearing. What the Russians couldn't use was burned. Houses, shops, sacks of bones wrapped in mutilated skin.

We had done nothing wrong, or so we thought. But that was not the worst of it. I do not remember too many details about the days and weeks of October and November. But I do remember December 10th. That was the day our village was changed forever.

CHAPTER 3

The old Ukrainian turned silent. The fire in his eyes vanished. His stare was now cold, lifeless. A very dead kind of nothing.

It was the look Geoff had seen so many times at the Rockefeller. Mental patients who had absorbed so much of the world's pain that they retreated behind their own walls.

But L. Geoffrey Weinburg, Ph.D., M.D., didn't come halfway around the world to see another catatonic psychiatric patient stare his life away. There were a lot of dollars, rubles, and deutschmarks behind this investigation. There was also the matter of personal reputation.

"You're hiding something from me. Or you're laughing at me. NO one laughs at me. NO one," Geoff said. He refused to raise his voice. NO one was going to see him lose control.

Still, the catatonic stare. It was an old stumbling block Yakov had rammed his head against so many times. Yakov shook his head, then offered a prayer to the God scientists are allowed to pray to.

"He told me what happened next. Once," Yakov related. "He was in a good mood and trusted me that day. Then,   when I brought in my supervisors for verification..."

"Five milligrams haloperidol," Geoff interrupted. No curse from Hell or Heaven was immune to the power of psychoactive drugs. It was a personal challenge. No psychotic preacher or schizophrenic New Age visionary passed through Geoff's psychiatric service without coming out with HIS construct of reality. "Five milligrams of haloperidol!!" he repeated.

The command was ignored by Igor Trotivoi, an orderly with the loyalty of a fine dog, and more medical knowledge than most of the physicians he worked under. "Five milligrams of haloperidol," Geoff repeated again in Russian. "It will go into YOU or HIM."

Igor stood firm. The Ukrainian faded further into the world behind his glassy eyes. Geoff steamed with anger.

Yakov nodded to Igor. Prayer, with a few cc's of science, might be the prescription that was needed.

Igor had the build of a Russian bear on steroids. Nothing on two legs could stop him. Except a Ukrainian possessed by demons - or an angel awakened from his slumber.

Igor found himself on the floor with three broken ribs. Boris ended his shift with a swift kick out the door, then ensured Igor's non-return by bolting the steel door shut. Yakov reached for the alarm, but not before Boris pulled the wires out of the wall. Geoff had seen psych patients interconvert from Woody Allan to the Incredible Hulk before, but no brand of PCP that he knew was this powerful.

Boris' eyes focused on Geoff, like a hawk hovering over a paralyzed mouse. Geoff was not used to being hunted. It was new. And terrifying. A cracked neck. An overdose of haloperidol. Or both.

Terror was new to Geoff. So was pissing in his hundred dollar trousers. Boris smiled. The first lesson was learned. Geoff was ready for some more teaching. And it was time for the full story to be told.

Reel 3

The Bolsheviks were remaking the map of the Soviet Republics, and by some political blunder, or divine accident, Telenkov was to be a central supply junction. The nearest railroad was still two days' walk or half a day's ride away. However, machinery from Moscow no longer needed tracks. Trucks could move over the Steppes, as long as they had enough gasoline, and it was not mud or deep snow season. They could almost outrun a good horse, and could certainly carry more cargo. Why we were not carted away with those trucks to labor camps, we would never know. Perhaps it was a blessing. Perhaps a curse. Nadia always said the world worked that way, particularly in Telenkov.

We were promised food if we worked hard at maintaining the supply line, which robbed Ukraine of food, resources, and, as we envisioned in the closed trucks, people. The harder we worked, the more the officers promised, and the less the guards delivered.

In command of our once-independent community was Major Mikhail Rusmonski. He was the most interesting Russian I ever met, and the most dangerous. "Beware of the Russians. They take your dignity away slowly, so it hurts more," Nicholi kept reminding me, as if he knew that it was I who had to realize that more than anyone else in Telenkov.

The Major always communicated to us through his staff and a translator. We lived in constant fear of what he was thinking behind his cold blue eyes.

The Russians always came for you when you were asleep. We learned very quickly to go to bed wearing our warmest clothes and boots. When they came for me, I did not ask "why." Perhaps it was wisdom, or fear. Both went hand in hand that winter. I did have the courage to ask "where?" "The Major wants to see you," one of the guards said. His voice was muffled, and in its own way, had as much fear in it as mine.

The walk down the main street was the longest I ever took without cuffs, blindfolds, or any gun in the small of my back. It felt more like an escort than an arrest. It was still November, I think. Were my friends looking at me with envy, contempt, or admiration? What did the Major know about me that was so important? I was just as unimportant as anyone else in Telenkov, and just as expendable.

I was allowed to knock on the door that had been the Town Hall. "Enter, please." It was the first time I heard "please" said to me in a long time.

I was blinded by the winter sun coming in through the window. A silhouetted man gazing outside spoke. "Beethoven's Opus 110. Can you play it?" The voice was soft and dangerously "kind." He cued me with the first few notes. Was it an ultimatum? Was I finally being found out for the crime of having a mother who taught me "intellectual" music? I didn't think that knowing how to play music written by someone else was special, and neither did anyone else in Telenkov.

I moved closer. A violin was on the table, a cup of tea, and a nut-raisin cake next to it. My body told me to fill my stomach. My mind - and burning curiosity - made me grab the violin. I struck the first fortissimo notes, hard and fast.

My host turned around, went to a piano, and played. He sat straight at attention, but his long fingers were in tune with the music of the universe. By the fifth measure, the Major and I were talking with the Spirit of Beethoven. By the tenth, we were speaking to each other's hearts.

By the fifth Sonata, we were the best of friends. I had forgotten that he was a Russian officer, and he had forgotten that I was a Ukrainian "comrade" serving the Soviet Republic. There was just the music.

That was all I remembered from the first day I met the Major. That, and the cake and sausage he gave me to take home.

My Ukrainian friends shared the cake, though there was scarcely a biteful for each of them. The Soviets knew that a starving man with a little food does not rebel, but a starving man with no food has nothing to lose, making him prime fuel for a counter-revolution, you see.

The guards took away the sausage. They had more important plans for it, involving the company dog, "Putz."

The soldiers hated Putz as much as they hated us. He was really the Major's dog. The shepherd-wolf cross had found its way into the Major's mess hall when he was stationed near Kiev, then into the Major's heart, then into the company ranks. Though the animal had teeth sharper than a gypsy's tongue, he never learned to kill for his food.

He was a useless animal, as the soldiers saw things. They named him Putz, convincing the Major that the name meant "mighty warrior" in an obscure Lithuanian dialect.

To relieve the boredom of their sadistic and miserable lives, the soldiers played a game with Putz. They would put food into the dog's mouth and then grab it back, just before the emaciated animal had a chance to swallow it. It was a timed event, with a set of rules that changed every time the judge became drunker. Captain Joseph Korsikov was the winner every time.

Korsikov was tired of his audience of Russian recruits, so he assigned us to be his admiring crowd. He brought Putz and the sausage to the tavern, a place where we all met at noon every day to discuss life, but now a place we used to silently contemplate death together, in the hope that it would have some meaning.

Korsikov was alone, daring us to jump him. He knew we wouldn't, and he never let us forget it. Not as long as he had food in his deep pockets and a Red Star on his lapel.

"Come here, Putz," Korsikov said to the dog. The animal edged up, tail between his legs for another licking he was sure to get. "Come here," he continued. There was a twisted smile on his face that even fooled us, as our mouths watered for a morsel of the sausage bait.

Putz was in worse shape than we were. Starving him was a source of amusement for the soldiers. They told the Major that Putz had a medical condition that made him thin, no matter how much he ate.

Putz approached Korsikov slowly. The Captain smiled. His right hand was extended, open, the sausage in it, its odor enriched by a touch of mustard. The other hand was behind his back, ready to crack a whip over the dog's half-broken back. Korsikov knew that Putz needed the meat and that the dog had forfeited his dignity for survival many times before.

"Time this one," Korsikov screamed out as Putz reached for the sausage. We knew that the meat would wind up in Korsikov's mouth and that Putz would go hungry again. It pained us, particularly because it was US who kept Putz alive with the scraps of food we could spare. It was something we knew that we had to do.

Korsikov leaned back, prepared to teach the dog another lesson in how to become helpless. Putz seemed more helpless than on most days. Korsikov let down his guard. We let our hopes sink.

Putz slowly closed his jaws around the sausage, giving Korsikov more than enough time to pull it out of the dog's mouth. But Putz was after a bigger meal than pork wieners.

It takes courage to bite the hand that feeds you, and Putz was a courageous dog that day. We had our first silent communal laugh in a long time, watching Korsikov with a mouth full of dog teeth in his arm.

Korsikov screamed in agony, then panic, neither expression giving credit to his rank as Captain in the bravest Army in the world. Putz released his grip. The dog looked at Korsikov's angry eyes, then at the sausage on the floor. He took the wiener, refusing to swallow it. He showed it off to Korsikov, daring the Captain to try and take it from HIM. However, Korsikov was not interested in any game where he was not guaranteed to win.

Korsikov could only grunt. "I'll kill you, you...." He grabbed his whip and cracked it, catching nothing but air with its tip. Putz ran off to the woods, sausage in his mouth and pride in his stride.

Korsikov pulled out his revolver. We pulled back our laughter. However, Korsikov did not temper his anger.

He fired into the woods. Once, twice, then three times. The winter cold sharpened the sound of his bullets. A howl of pain from the woods drove shivers up our already frostbitten bodies. Horror went through all of us, simultaneously, somehow.

"YOU did it," Korsikov told us. "YOU shot the Major's dog, and when he finds out, you will all pay. You AND your children."

We had seen too many children with smiling faces and swollen bellies, their ever-hopeful eyes bulging out of their heads. Whether they were our own or someone else's didn't matter anymore. They had taken to eating leaves, so their stomachs could feel full before they threw up, or worse. The field mice were gone, and some had taken to killing nightingales, our National bird. It was a bad omen to kill nightingales. They were our Spirit protectors. But our souls were now worth less than a mouthful of meat. We valued ourselves that little.

What we did next, we did for ourselves and our children. Korsikov pushed too far. We had nothing to lose but our humiliation.

We all remembered that day, from the inside. Our hearts were in our knotted stomachs. Our hands on every part of the Captain, inflicting as much pain on him as possible. Even Father - now Comrade - Dimitri found his fist around Korsikov's throat, his teeth gritted with satisfaction.

We stepped over the line, into a realm where God's morality did not limit us. Finally, our fate was in our own hands now, and it scared the hell out of us.

CHAPTER 4

Boris' beet-red face turned white. He was not used to being so reflective at times of urgency. For all his faults, Boris was a man of action. He was now paralyzed. Terrorized with a secret that was far more horrifying than hunger, murder, or abandonment of a God who had guided his village for centuries.

"And..." Geoff said. "I need details. The U. S. State Department tells me OFFICIALLY that thousands of people are in danger of a new communicable disease. The unofficial story I've heard is that it's a lot bigger than that. You talk, I can fix it. You clam up, and I go back home. Let you Soviets destroy your own country while I watch my colleagues at home destroy mine."

Still, more silence. Then, a catatonic stare from Boris into the wall.

Geoff had been on wild epidemiological goose chases before. And he had even been convinced by taller tales than this. Psychotic patients were very gifted, he thought. They could read your mind. Find secrets in there you never knew you had. And convince you that the strangest lies were the most common truths. Maybe Boris was a master hypnotist who finally lost his concentration. Maybe he was just another wacko who believed his delusions so much that he coerced you to follow him into Oz with him.

Yakov shook his head. "Defeated again," his eyes screamed out.

Geoff looked at his watch. "Our patient's time is up. And if your government doesn't need my services anymore..."

From Yakov, more deadening silence.

For Geoff, it was an interesting story. And a free trip. Although Geoff had six figures' worth of grant money set aside for travel, he still took advantage of free trips, a fringe benefit built into the job. After all, no one respects a man who doesn't steal what he can.

Geoff closed his briefcase, making it sound as loud as he could. "Gentlemen." His tone was civil, dignified. Boris' response was not.

Geoff found himself tossed against the wall, a wrinkled hand against his throat. "You WILL listen to me. You WILL listen."

Yakov tried to pull Boris off. But the strength of madness was far more powerful than that of reason. Boris had been transformed into a rabid animal. Nothing could stop him from killing his prey. Nothing except one word.

"The children," Yakov said. "The children."

Boris froze. His rage transformed into guilt, then regret, then helplessness. Geoff always stayed away from men - and even women - who were reduced to tears. Yakov instinctually went to their aid.

Yakov spoke some encouraging words to Boris. The kind of words that needed no translation. They were enough to restore Boris's composure and dignity.

"The end is close for him. We don't have much time left," Yakov whispered to Geoff. "I've seen it happen like this with the others, too."

"The others?" Geoff asked.

"All dead now. I think. Or dying somewhere I don't know about."

"What the fuck is all this about, Yakov?!!!."

"Right now, it's about listening. For both of us. But if YOU want to go home to a safe and predictable life..."

Yakov was determined. He knew that calling Geoff out on a dare was a low blow. Dare Geoff to "get a life," and you had him by the balls.

For better or worse, Geoff was hooked. In ways that he had not yet even realized. In a conspiracy that dealt with the heart of the collective Soviet soul. There was no choice but to put on the next reel, give Boris another cigarette, and venture into a forbidden area of Oz not reachable by the yellow brick road.

Reel 5

We were transformed into animals. Worse than animals. Me, Father Dimitri, Nicholi, Sergei, and even the women.

Each of us wanted some part of Korsikov. Father Dimitri went for the throat, like the savage pagan barbarians who sacked the Holy Cathedrals in Rome and Constantinople.

Nicholi grabbed the testicles, twisting the sperm cord around his bloody hand. Tasha pulled out Korsikov's eyeballs with a stick and her frostbitten fingers. The vicious demons that had possessed Korsikov's eyes found their way into hers that day. I found myself clawing at the left arm, I think. We ripped it out of the socket, then hacked it off with rusty picks. Someone ripped out the heart, someone else plucked out the lungs. Pieces of liver were on most everyone else's hands.

The children were outside. We kept them away from the tavern meetings. They were entitled to know what would happen to them, but they also had a right to have a childhood, pathetic and short as it was in those times. They were not as horrified of starvation as we adults were. At least it seemed that way. They still knew how to laugh. We wondered if we could ever laugh again.

The carnage continued, centuries of oppression unleashed in two minutes of mad rage. Only one of us was immune from the curse.

Anna watched. She had as much reason to hate Korsikov as any of us. Maybe more.

A woman in Anna's profession could do well in bad times, as long as she respected herself and knew the value of her services. Anna had the conviction - and insight - to demand the full asking price from ANY Bolshevik customer. Korsikov knew that for a few extra rubles, he could secure Anna's passion, maybe even love.

The arrangement had worked for the first three visits. Anna learned to understand, even empathize with a secret part of Korsikov. A part of the sadistic bastard's background that he kept hidden, even from himself. It was a gift she had, getting into the heart of even the coldest customer. She seemed part nun and part whore. It was her greatest strength, and most vulnerable weakness.

By the fourth visit, Korsikov had gotten tired of both passion and love. He extracted a "tuition" fee from Anna for teaching her how a first-class Russian Captain makes love to a third-class Hungarian gypsy whore. Her entire life savings would do for the first payment. A lashing on the back for the second.

It was something that always happened to Anna, wherever she went. The path of an honorable outlaw.

That journey started early in life. Anna was brought up in a strict, Orthodox family, and almost became a Nun. Her first sexual experience was an accident of passion. She explained it to me once, in private, with words I will always remember.

"When he stroked my cheek, I thought I was making love to a Guardian Angel. When he kissed my lips, I felt the love of God flowing between us. I surrendered to him, and he surrendered to me. It was like touching Jesus. Afterward, I realized that he was just a man. A pathetic man who was bored with his wife. And his daughter." She told her feelings to her mother, then to the priest. "I did it because all the other girls did it. Or at least they say they did."

Anna was complimented for her honesty. Then rewarded with a pair of shackles, a vacation in a sanitarium, a shaved head, and a reputation she could never live down, no matter how many Nunneries she joined.

Anna lived the rest of her childhood alone, as an outlaw, then a gypsy. Maybe it was because her first "Jesus" was an influential man who wanted to remain so. But it was only a matter of time before Anna would be exiled from those who lived within boundaries. She quickly learned the only real rule about life for people like her - "if you live outside the law, you have to be honest." It was a very important rule, especially if you're not smart about your feelings.

But Anna was wise when it came to other people's feelings. "What are we going to tell the Major?" she said, as our growls and groans quieted down enough for our ears to be open. Korsikov's body was scattered all over the floor, too big to be swept under the rug, and too gruesome to be kept out of our minds.

On the fateful day when we had to decide what to do about Koriskov's remains, Anna related the facts to us that had to be considered in whatever solution we chose, or which chose us. The ground was too hard to dig into, the snow was not deep enough to bury even a small corpse, and the river was being watched by armed guards day and night. Not even a gopher could pass by without being noticed and asked for transport permits.

We were now outlaws, and not very good ones. We argued, agonized, and worried. I nervously looked out the window at a convoy passing through. It carried more guns than I had ever seen.

My reason, then conscience, was held hostage by fear. I hoped—and prayed—that the machine guns would be used on some other village. It was a shameful thought, but one I couldn't deny.

I heard footsteps behind me. Retribution already, I thought, for our desperate needs and our shameful thoughts. I turned around, my heart in my stomach, prepared to face my Creator - and Executioner. What I saw turned out to be the beginning of something far more horrifying than death or eternal damnation.

Putz decided to come back from the woods. Korsikov's bullet grazed his shoulder, but he wanted a rematch. He licked the blood oozing from Korsikov's wrist, then worked his way up the arm for a more substantial meal. One decisive bite into the elbow and the dog ripped off a bone, thick, juicy, and succulent.

The wood stove still had an hour of heat left in it.

The Russians were always kind enough to leave us pots and pans, so we could notice what we couldn't fill them with. They also allowed us just enough time together to argue about our immediate problems, but not enough for us to devise any long-term solutions.

I heard somewhere that human meat tastes like chicken. And we all knew that there was a special kind of madness and suffering that all children went through before they died of starvation. Those were the only two thoughts that went through my mind as we men carved up Korsikov's body with our trembling hands. The women steamed it in closed pots with melted snow.

We didn't speak a word. Even Father Dimitri was silent, the saint-like beard that covered his mouth stained with Korsikov's blood.

Nicholi spoke. "Better the children not know about this. Our job is to worry. Their job is to stay alive."

Nicholi was one of the only men over the age of 20 who was not a father. He said it was because he could never commit himself to a family. "One day my Cossack ancestors will call me," he would say. "I'll get on my horse, put on my Grandfather's sheepskin vest, ride all the way to Vladiovostok, gaze out at the Pacific Ocean, and never come back."

It was a trip he never took. I never saw anyone so tied to Telenkov, or someone who wanted to father a child so much. Maybe it was because Nicholi feared happiness. Struggle was the only thing he knew, and if women eased the pain of struggle, having children would kill his spirit. Still, no one was more generous with gifts at Christmas, and no one was better at keeping small children spell-bound with bigger-than-life stories about Spirits and Angels.

"We'll tell the children that we're bringing home wild chicken," Nicholi proposed.. "Magical chickens from Saint George and the Elk people in the Northern Mountains. It's a magical secret they have to keep. Or the Elk people will have to return to their home in the center of the earth, something that will make them very sad, because they haven't seen the sun in two thousand years. Their gift loses magic if anyone knows about it." Most of us nodded. Nicholi was imaginative yet logical. "You just had to think like a child, something which I found very difficult, even when I was growing up." He continued.

"By eating the meat from the magic chickens, your souls will learn how to fly. But only if you keep it a secret. Otherwise, your feet will be stuck to the earth, and you'll never get a chance to fly above the Northern Horizon, to ride with Saint George and the Elk Riders as they slay the dragons of evil." I think Nicholi was believing the story himself. I know I was starting to. But some clung on to another kind of mythology.

"Saint George serves God, not Pagans," Father Dimitri protested. "When the children ask us where we got this meat, we won't answer them. Tell them it was a gift from God, and that the devil will kill them if they disobey their parents and ask more questions."

"They're ten pounds away from death already," Nicholi retorted, without losing a beat.

"The older children aren't going to believe this Pagan storytale."

"But they are smart enough to let the younger ones believe in it. Older children know when to stop believing in dreams and fables, and that younger ones need them."

Checked, but not checkmated, Father Dimitri persisted. "Only the fear of God can still save them. And us."

"The hope of something beyond heaven or hell is their only real salvation," Nicholi countered.

"God will save us. If we remain faithful, Nicholi."

"God is a sadist. And He doesn't even know it!!!"

"Damn you to hell, Nicholi. Damn you to..."

"Shhh," Tasha interrupted. Her tone said it all. Nicholi and Father Dimitri had their entire lives to fight over who would be the spiritual leader. Besides, she had her fill of men who wanted to be spiritual or political leaders. For that matter, she was tired of men in general. All things considered, I could not blame her.

After a well-deserved meal of Korsikov delight, Putz left. He realized that it was time to let humans decide the fate of other humans. Besides, his place was with the Major. The Major was certainly not the sanest of masters, but he was compassionate, consistent, and loyal.

Captain Korsikov's legacy was little more than the gray-brown flesh burning in our pots. His gun was an 1885 Navy Colt, captured from the American Expeditionary Forces in the Civil War of 1919. The barrel was rusty, and even if we could get ammunition to fit the chamber, it was God's call as to which direction the bullet would fire if we pulled the trigger. In Korsikov's wallet was the obligatory photo of Comrade Stalin, and three days' wages. No pictures or letters from family, sweethearts or friends.

"No one is going to miss Korsikov," Anna commented. "He was a loner. He was not connected to anyone or anything. He was a pathetic bastard not important enough for God, the devil, or the Elk Rider Spirits to care about."

Anna's words were vicious and sympathetic. They could have referred to herself as much as the Bolshevik Captain, who nearly stole what was left of her self-respect. There was still a lot about Anna's past that we didn't know. I knew more than others, yet every answer I could figure out about Anna's past only brought up ten more questions.

But Anna's past as an outlaw and Korsikov's future in any afterlife were not on our minds. Survival was. Survival of our bodies and souls. We valued them both, thank God.

Anna pointed out some obvious things to us that the Soviets mistrusted us as much as we hated them. That their weapons were always loaded and within a second's reach. That they were naked without their weapons, and their warm wool uniforms. And that the only time they were without either was in her company.

There were some interesting complications which, when viewed from an optimist's perspective, were unused opportunities. The Major had few orders he strictly enforced, but fraternization with Ukrainian women was one of them. Maybe it was a code of honor passed down to him by his father, a Cavalry Officer who saved Mother Russia from the Turks, Chinese and Japanese in "honorable" wars that the world would never see again. The Major belonged to a past era - a time of chivalry, when Knights were pure of heart and every woman went to the altar a virgin. Or maybe the Major had a paternal obsession with racial purity, obliging him to keep Northern Russia free from contamination by inferior Ukrainian bloodlines, and vice versa.

It was hard to figure out whether the Major was motivated by kindness, hatred or ignorance. But one thing was certain. The penalty for any soldier getting caught with Anna was expulsion to Siberia, to camps that were even worse than those reserved for Ukrainian counter-revolutionaries.

Arresting Anna would have been easy, but the Major believed that it was inappropriate and unnecessary. After all, Anna did give her word to the Major that she would restrict her activities to Ukrainian clients, a pledge that had been delivered with Korsikov's pistol embedded into the small of her back. And, after all, in Korsikov's world, a soldier's word was his bond.

When all was said and NOT done, Anna's trade was booming. There was no shortage of soldiers who wanted to mock the Major by defying the no-fraternization order. Besides, a lifetime in Siberia was worth a night in Anna's company, as evidenced by the rows of soldiers who spouted a third leg every time she sauntered down the streets. A glance would drive them mad. A lilting wave from her flowing, slender fingers would make them wet their trousers. It did not please Tasha to have to do so much laundry for the soldiers, but she needed the morsels of food they gave her for the services and silence.

Some say that Nicholi was Anna's pimp, but he was more like an older brother. I know that he would have liked to have been a lot closer. But once Anna said "no," particularly to a friend,
it was final. She knew how to give love to more than one man. Nicholi, for all his boasting, only knew how to give loyalty to one woman. At the very least, a professional career or a life would have been lost if passions were allowed a free rein.

The most important fact now was that we had all become murderers. We were soon to become worse.

Nicholi took a chunk out of what had been Korsikov's arm. He took a bite. His eyes were dispassionate, but not cruel.

"It needs a little basil and oregano. Besides, I can negotiate a deal with God. God will ignore the fact that I'm eating meat on Friday, and I'll ignore that He got drunk one day and created Bolsheviks." Nicholi's joke was not appreciated. His follow-up comment was.

"We're playing according to their rules now. There will be more killing. But the most evil one should die first. For the rest of Ukraine. The categorical imperative. And the collective good of humanity in relation to the God-Head it's connected to." We didn't know or understand what our self-taught, over-read, and self-appointed "philosopher king" meant by God-Head and categorical imperative. But his real meaning was clear enough. "The most evil should die first."

"Who are we to judge who deserves to die?" Father Dimitri challenged. "Only God can know how much good or evil is in the hearts of men. Can YOU look into the eyes of another person and know, for certain, if he deserves to live or die? If he deserves to have his life taken? Is a life based on killing others who may be innocent worth living?"

"These soldiers might have families like ours in Russia," Elena added.

"And just because they are Russian, that doesn't mean they are Soviets," Tasha added.

A communal moment of reflection overcame us. Then more arguing. No one ever won an argument in Telenkov, except the one who walked away first.

I felt my mouth possessed by an intelligence far greater than my own. The words came out. "Anna could help us find out who deserves to live or die. God is dead, or sleeping. It's our turn to take His place." A profound silence overtook the room. I looked over to Anna. She had been thinking the same thing. The solution was simple, bold, and crazy. We would follow it, despite the silent warning Anna gave us with her terrified eyes.

CHAPTER 5

"Another cigarette," Boris said to Geoff. "Please."

Geoff complied. Tales of cannibalism fascinated him. It was the only violation of good taste that still could.

On more than one occasion, he would rent a movie about the Donner Party, or some other flick where white people eat other white people. Refreshments would be served at the appropriate time, steak and ribs with red barbecue sauce. Geoff would comment on how human flesh smelt, tasted, and felt, using cold medical, or crueler non-medical, language to bring his narration to life.

More than one groupie, colleague, or lover left a green trail of vomit on the way out of Geoff's house and his life. It was fun, and a "test." Only those with a strong sense of humor could survive the dog-eat-dog world.

"We have some drawings. Sketches," Yakov said to Geoff while he was in mid-thought.

Geoff always flipped past the art section in the Sunday Times. Any interest he had in painting was confined to how easily he could score with the artist. But there was something about the strokes of the pencil in Boris' sketches, the shading under the eyes, the depth of even the wrinkleless faces. They moved something very human in Geoff.

This was not the work of an accomplished artist, but undoubtedly the product of an experienced man. There was something about Boris in each of the characters, in the eyes, ears, nose, or hands.

"The 'primitive' school. When did he draw these?" Geoff inquired, hiding behind whatever cultural superiority he still could hold on to.

"You mean, WHY did he draw them?" Yakov asserted.

"Yakov. Don't fuck around! We're investigating an epidemic here. A specific disease this guy has. I want to know WHAT this thing is, WHERE it's located, and WHO'S spreading it. I'll give you five minutes to tell me the 'what', 'who', and 'where's' of these sketches."

"If both of us don't find out the 'WHY', the 'who', 'where', and 'what' won't matter. Are you really that stupid!!!?"

"I may be a moron to you idiots, but I am one pissed off motherfucker right now!!!"

"So am I!"

Boris gave them a round of applause. "Passion is good for the soul. Particularly the soul of you scientists," he said.

Boris presented them with a quick sketch, drawn while the cream of Soviet and American science were arguing like spoiled schoolboys. The Ukrainian's hand was skillful enough to catch their best qualities, in a cartoon that could easily fetch a C-note at a Soho auction.

Geoff cracked a smile. He enjoyed laughing at himself, a pleasure he seldom indulged in, because deep down he still thought everyone else was laughing at him. No matter how many Nobel prizes he got, there would still be someone from the old neighborhood laughing at him. And the ghost of his father would keep demanding that he get 110% on every exam life made him take. Geoff hated his father for intimidating him into greatness, and loved him for it.

Yakov was raised to be aristocratic, not arrogant. As the son of Party-approved Russian intelligentsia, he put value on what he was, as well as what he did. It was what made Yakov enjoy his accomplishments and his life. Appreciating what life gave you, instead of longing for what the fates had taken, was a survival skill inbred into the Russian psyche.

"We're losing time," Boris said. The alarm clicked down. "By tonight, they're coming for me. Tomorrow, they'll come for you. BOTH of you."

Geoff looked at Yakov. "Did someone forget to tell me something, Yakov?"

"We want freedom. We get chaos. Then terror. Because we always let very quiet people stay in control," Yakov replied. "They have as much to lose if the real story leaks out as we do."

"Who? The Alluminati? The Klan? A Trump-mediated merger of the fuckin KGB and the goddamn CIA? Who's behind this?"

"We can beat them with the truth. We have to find out the truth."

"Come on, you're not fuckin' Harrison Ford and this is not a fucking movie. This is real life, Yakov."

"Yes. It is."

Yakov's answer was succinct, uncompromising.

It was Boris's turn to express the urgency of the moment with words. "Now, we talk about the 'whys'? Unless you understand WHY it all happened, the rest of the facts will make no sense at all," Boris said. He put the tape recorder on.

Geoff listened. Yakov prayed that Boris would tell the story again. It was too horrible and ironic to be made up by the human mind, and there were bound to be sideplots added which would not make the listening any easier. Maybe the whole account of events was a hoax, Yakov thought. He knew it was wishful thinking, and prepared himself for the worst.

Reel 6

Moral dilemmas were a part of life in Telenkov, and we did not know how to live without them. Guilt is the sin of those with an inflated conscience, and we relished in it.

It stemmed from a conflict of loyalties, again. Our children needed food, and needed us to be alive for them next winter. By that time, the Bolshevik nightmare would be over, one way or another. We would all be sitting together in Heaven or a rebuilt Telenkov, which seemed to be the same thing.

The hope of ANY afterlife better than this one was a thought that was in the back of the mind of every Christian, even the Atheists. The Jews, I was told by Nadia the gypsy, did not believe in an afterlife. They lived life for today and valued what they could leave behind. To be forgotten was to be eternally dead. To the Jews, DISbelief strengthened the human spirit. It was all too strange, perhaps too uncomfortable, for me to believe. And most of us in that room, rightly or wrongly, were still Christians.

Nicholi was the only real atheist amongst us, and it was to him that we turned for spiritual guidance. "Everyone should taste a bite here, so that you won't get upset in front of the children." He was right about that. He was wrong in insisting that Father Dimitri take the first bite.

"For the children," Nicholi repeated, as Father Dimitri stared at the brown flesh in front of him. It must have taken a lot of courage for our Priest to take a large mouthful of human flesh, or the complete absence of courage. I still don't know.

"God will be even more vengeful to us because today is Friday," Father Dimitri moaned, meat having never passed his lips on a Friday since an accidental tasting of what he thought was whitefish stew five years ago.

"We aren't eating meat," Nicholi countered. "We're eating RUSSIAN. Russians are lower than animals. Lower than radishes."

Nicholi knew that we needed more convincing. He used logic this time. "Killing Korsikov may have been a sin. But eating him is a far lesser sin. He felt more pain when we ripped his throat open than when we boiled his neck in a soup pot. He felt more agony when we punched into his guts than when we used them to make sausages."

Nicholi was always a pragmatist, and underneath all the yelling and screaming, the most logical man I've ever met. It was logical to kill Russians who would kill our children, and it was logical to use their bodies to feed hungry people. For Telenkov to stay alive, we had to survive.

What we didn't anticipate was how different we would feel once we crossed over into a world governed by the affairs of man, rather than the rules laid down by God. Sergei felt strong in some way after the first bite and even took a second. Elena nibbled and pretended to swallow it. Johan felt completely detached from his body, mind, and spirit. He didn't know what he was becoming. I just felt numb. The numb that is neither life, nor death. Tasha reacted in a very different way.

"We didn't have the food blessed first," she said. "God would have forgiven us if we blessed it first. Even Saint Peter can't save it now."

"How SEVERE is the sin?" Johan offered. "Those of us who took ten bites of the Captain's flesh will have to repent to the Virgin Mary for ten years, those who took five bites, only five years." Johan had a big mouth, of course, and the thought of a God who did not match the severity of sins with gradations of punishment was beyond his conception. After all, Heaven was built like the Polish court system, or was it the other way around?

We argued again, everyone taking a side, often switching sides in mid-sentence. I even found myself yelling, my mouth very disconnected from my mind and heart.

Anna cleared her throat. It was time to reveal the plan she had been thinking of, but I was only imagining. "The Miller's Cottage," she said just loud enough for us to hear it. She was referring to the shack outside town, where boys got experienced and men satisfied for as long as anyone could remember.

A serene and affirmative silence came over the room. It was a strange silence, one which I would never forget. Somehow, all of us were thinking the same thing, and not disagreeing on it. Ukrainians working together - an ideal we boasted about to Russians and Poles, but never experienced ourselves.

No one lived in the Miller's Cottage since the Tartar invasion, but it was Nicholi's unwritten responsibility to keep it in good condition, a task for which he was paid very good wages in the most valuable Telenkovian currency - tolerance of his unintelligible eccentricities and excesses of passion. The wooden bedboard was free of bats and mice. Mattresses of straw and feathers were kept dry and louse-free, even in the wettest summer. The walls kept out the cold winter wind, but the cracks allowed viewing by those with small eyes and big curiosities.

Nicholi had extracted some payment from Anna in the form of services to maintain the Miller's Cottage in good condition. But even Nicholi was not immune to jealousy. "An attic. You need a good attic to keep the rains from coming down. A good roof is not enough," Nicholi kept arguing.

Anna gave in, finally, and enjoyed having two solid walls over her head when all the rest of us barely had one. She also had uninvited visitors in the attic, in the form of mice, squirrels and wild foxes, some of which walked on two legs. Anna knew Nicholi had a good view of her bed below from his place above her, but it didn't bother her. Or so she let Nicholi believe, on so many occasions that frustrated him to no end.

Nicholi made the attic big, sparing no expense. A special feature was hidden viewing windows, set up with mirrors. Like a submarine periscope in reverse, you could look into the corner of the ceiling and see everything on the bed below. Pinecone insulation in the walls could absorb the groans and moans of any viewer. There was room for at least seven people to look down below and enough pinecones to absorb twenty arguments, thirty if the wind was strong and the windows were cracked open.

Logic and moral imperatives seldom co-existed in Telenkov, but were ominously the same that winter. We couldn't bear to hug our children anymore and feel their ribs on our own emaciating bodies. What we would do to the Soviet soldiers would be for our children. How we would do it would be for us.

"The most evil must die first," Father Dimitri reminded us. It was the only thing we agreed on, but it was the most important thing. The problem - evil is in the eye of the beholder. For centuries we were so busy judging ourselves, and always coming up with a guilty verdict, that the prospect of judging someone else, and perhaps finding them innocent, was foreign. Would, or could, we actually find some people NOT worthy of dying by our hand?

In war, such decisions were made for us. You shoot at whoever is shooting at you. War is chaos, where God forgives transgressions. But peacetime, harsh as it was then, was just as chaotic and cruel, or so we tried to convince ourselves.

CHAPTER 6

An alarm went off. A loud screech penetrated through Geoff's skull. Outside, a squadron of jeeps crept up over the hill. Soldiers in mud-soaked combat gear with bright Red Stars on their lapels approached the head of the hand-picked multinational guard unit around the complex.

"Regular Army." Yakov said, looking out the window casually. "They're out here on manoeuvers. They shoot up some trees, maybe a deer or two, and call it military manoeuvers. Patrolling the woods makes them still feel useful. After a bottle of vodka and a few war stories, they'll be on their way."

Yakov opened a box on the wall and adjusted the wiring inside. The alarm signal outside stopped. The one in Boris' head kicked into hyperdrive.

"You said it's fixed," Boris said to Yakov. "You promise to fix alarm system, and I promise to tell you story."

Boris put out his cigarette, burnt down only half way. It was the "session over" signal, firmly given to the shrinks, government investigators, and close friends alike. Right now, Yakov was some combination of all three in Boris' eyes, and until he was sure of how well Yakov could deliver on his promises, the interview was over.

"I want to go to my room now," Boris demanded. Yakov had no choice but to accommodate the request, or apologize. He did neither.

"You ARE in your fucking room now," the former Muscovite screamed through gritted teeth. Yakov's right hand pressed against Boris' throat, with the old man's back rammed against the wall.

Yakov had never raised a finger against another human being, even for show. He had avoided conscription in the Soviet Army because he was smart enough to qualify for the most prestigious biomedical scientist training in Moscow. He avoided being assigned to a mainstream Soviet research post by being clever enough to get a post-doctoral fellowship in New York. Yakov pledged that upon his return he would, if asked, devote his work toward helping the Soviet people, a euphemism that usually had more implications for National Security than medical need.

It was a gamble, maybe a stupid one. Another was letting a lifetime of frustration out on a Ukrainian who hated the Soviet systems as much as he did. The easiest way to shut Boris' mouth up tight was to threaten to kill him if he didn't talk. Yakov knew it, but pressed on anyway, exerting as much pain as he could without killing the old man.

Suddenly - shots from outside. A goose fell from the sky. The drunkest of the Soviet training troops put away his gun, poured the better part of a bottle of vodka down his throat, and shot up in the air again. "The Red Army Forever," he screamed out in desperation, as his slightly more sober Comrades pulled him into a jeep and drove back into the woods.

"Cigarette?" Geoff asked Boris.

The old Ukrainian was more suspicious than ever now. Why had Yakov brought over an American to solve a Russian-Ukrainian problem? And why THIS one? Geoff Weinburg had no real command of any language other than English. He had no understanding of the human condition outside the East Side ivy towers or below the Aspen ski slopes. Not a person who could be liked or trusted.

Yakov was no prize either. Who knew how many compromises he had to make to survive, in a world dominated on one side by well-armed Marxists and on the other by well-stocked Capitalists? Whenever Yakov spoke, it was with an honest heart. But his language was very formal-legalistic and scientific. And he always looked guilty about something. Maybe about something he did. Maybe about something he didn't do.

Still, Geoff knew enough to offer Boris a cigarette. "Yakov gives me false protection, and you, Lorie Geoffrey Weinburg, give me a cigarette. Maybe you think I'm a wise old Indian who you honor with sacred tobacco. Or maybe you just think I'm a stupid old redskin who you can buy with a black market cigarette."

Boris hesitated, then took the smoke. He moved it toward his mouth, slowly, and took a puff. Geoff pushed the record button on.

"One cigarette, one more tape. THEN you take me back to my room." Boris' demand was final.

Silent apologies having been made through gritted teeth and firm stares, Boris continued.

Reel 7

Lieutenant Reminkol never walked down the street, he strode, with a goose-step that intimidated everyone around him. His eyes were small, hidden deep in the sockets of a ghostlike skull. They would invite you to take a closer look, then trap you into a web of evil from which there was no escape, even in death.

Reminkol was a small man, in the way of the 19th century. He was at least three inches shorter than any other Bolshevik officer, and his frail bones made him look more like an underfed chicken than a man who had been in the Army for most of his adult life. And as for his manhood, that seemed questionable. There was the way he held a cigarette - with filter - between the third finger and thumb. He was obsessed with neatness, even during mud season. Then there was the lisp in his voice, a high pitch that came whining out of his small, sharply defined lips.

But in the ways of the 20th century, Reminkol was a man of high stature. Rumor had it that he was more powerful than any other Lieutenant in the Ukraine. The fact was that he had more power than any Major south of Leningrad.

Reminkol was a master of intimidation. He didn't need rank, money, or brute force to get what he wanted. From the tops of the hills we had called mountains as children, you could see the outlines of villages not too different from ours. After Reminkol did his inspection tours through them, all you could see was smoke. When the November winds blew over the Steppes, the stench of burning flesh permeated our frozen nostrils.

Lieutenant Reminkol had spent a few days at a time in Telenkov since the Bolshevik invasion. After Captain Korsikov had "deserted," Reminkol took his place as the only real military authority.

Naturally, we worried. Were we to be killed, our bodies mutilated beyond recognition, as was rapidly becoming the custom in "counter-revolutionary" villages? Were we to be shipped off to the Siberian labor camps in trains that seldom arrived with their full cargo of passengers? Or were we going to be kept alive so we could help the Bolsheviks kill Ukrainians from other villages?

We also pondered other matters. Was Reminkol really everything the legends said he was? Maybe he really was KGB, answerable only to Stalin. Or maybe he was the most effective liar in the Red Army, a small man who had bluffed his way into a position of power and security. Maybe he was protecting a family of his own, using the stories about how he could stab you in the back if you crossed him.

We were very bad at knowing who was evil by passion and who was cruel by necessity, particularly when it came to the Bolsheviks. Only God knew if Reminkol was destined for Heaven or Hell. Only we knew how dangerous he was on earth.

A few days after Korsikov met his inevitable end, Reminkol did his mid-day inspection of our work detail, on schedule, at ten AM sharp. We were enlisted to upgrade the roads through Telenkov so that Russian transport vehicles could get through. The trails had always been good enough for horses, but horses couldn't transport food, livestock, or people out of the Ukraine fast enough to please the Generals in Moscow.

"This road. Not wide enough." I can still remember the shrill of Reminkol's voice that day. "Thirty-five feet across," he related to the Sergeant in charge of the newly conscripted "Telenkov Volunteers."

"You said twenty-five feet yesterday," the Sergeant pointed out. The language was Russian, but the accent was Lithuanian, maybe Polish.

"Comrade Stalin's tanks are bigger today than yesterday!" Reminkol spat out. No one of inferior rank, or certainly of inferior national origin, had the right to talk back to a man who came from aristocratic blood lines which had kept Russian serfdom alive since the days of Ivan the Terrible.

Reminkol continued, "Sergeant. The road will be thirty-five feet wide tomorrow."

"Comrade Lieutenant. We need more machinery. More supplies. It's impossible to make the road thirty-five feet wide by tomorrow."

"Then you make it possible. Thirty-five feet. For Comrade Stalin's new tanks. Or be prepared to be reassigned."

"Reassignment" was the one word you didn't want to hear from Reminkol, and he applied that punishment to more than just the person in command. Either you found a way to do the impossible or deserted. The third choice was a living death somewhere very far from home.

I heard rumblings from the soldiers in the ranks. Languages other than Russian from men in Bolshevik uniforms. Spoken with fear, and a humanity not unlike our own. Elena was right. These people did have families, a long way from here. They were as afraid of never being able to go home as we were terrified of being taken away from ours.

But they were still Bolsheviks, armed and under orders to kill any of us without mercy. A bullet from a well-meaning Georgian conscript, trying to protect a family held hostage back home, was just as deadly as one from the pistol of a Bolshevik on an extermination hunt.

The Major wouldn't and couldn't help. He emerged out of his cloistered office only once a week, now guided around town by his second in command. Like Korsikov, Reminkol told the Major that trucks were coming in and out of the Telenkov daily, transporting badly needed food from collective farms that had excesses, to non-collectivized villages that were starving. Ukrainians were also being moved around, so they could get work and be united with their families, according to Reminkol's accounts.

I caught a look at the Major while he was being told the lies that his enemies in Moscow and his subordinates in Telenkov wanted him to believe. His eyes were open, but his mind was elsewhere. He soon stopped answering questions with directives and mandates, and reverted back to the only language he could really understand. Music was how he talked to the world. The madder things got, the harder he'd play. The crueler the punishments doled out to conscript soldiers and civilians, the more heartfelt the music from his window.

We got back to work, knowing that there was no way that the combined efforts of God, Saint George, and Comrade Stalin could ever lay down another ten mile stretch of road thirty-five feet wide. There was barely enough gravel to make a mile-long wagon trail, and the ground couldn't be broken apart with a diamond-headed pick.

Reminkol knew he was hated. He also wanted to be feared, some extra insurance. He knew the soldiers were cursing him in languages he couldn't understand. And he knew we were silently selling our own souls, in the hope that God would send him to Hell one day sooner than intended.

We found ourselves working with, or more often under, conscripts from all over the Soviet Union. They were better fed than us, but the soldiers still kept their weapons on them. They kept their distance, but they worked just as hard as we did trying to crack open the rock-hard winter ground with picks, shovels, and rusted knives.

Reminkol watched us work, and ate. It was a piece of fruit, I remember. An apple. I hadn't tasted an apple for months, or for that matter, eaten much of anything that resembled anything that a civilized person would call food.

Reminkol stood between us and survival, and he never let us forget it.

But we did have something far more powerful than God's wrath to use against Reminkol. Anna strolled by in a blue silk dress, cut low in front, slit down the side. In observance of the Major's request, she did cover her long blond hair with a shawl. But her eyes were inviting, her feet tightly wrapped by leather boots, making her look like a wild barbarian priestess who destroys her prey by drawing it into her cave. In her hands, shoes with three inch heels, both broken.

She sat next to the Lieutenant, rocks in one hand and nails in the other, requesting his assistance in shoe repair. She knew it would lead to the most important proposition she would ever make, as did we.

Ukrainian, Russian, and Bolshevik serfs alike turned their eyes down. I couldn't restrain myself from glancing up when I could. Neither could Nicholi. We were prepared to do whatever we had to do to protect Anna's honor, dignity, and survival, but we were pathetically helpless. We knew it, and she did too.

Reminkol offered Anna a bite out of his apple. He was polite, dignified. He seemed disinterested in her as a woman, but fascinated with her as a conquest. That was all the edge Anna needed.

"Isn't the woman supposed to tempt the man?" Anna said. She smiled, unleashing her hypnotic charms.

"Yes. The man is supposed to bite into the fruit of temptation first," Reminkol replied, as written in Anna's prewritten script.

It was Anna's move. She took the apple from Reminkol's hand. He went for his revolver, but stopped just before anyone but me could notice. She squeezed the apple, and let the juices run down the cleavage between her breasts. The pieces of fruit and seed dropped down that abyss into a black hole that sucked in Reminkol, driving him mad with passion. He moved in closer, prepared to dive as deep as he could and never come out.

One lick was enough to hook him. His breathing got heavy and his brow poured out sweat in the frigid deep-winter air.

Reminkol came up for air. Anna kissed him, under the neck. "Tonight. Ten o'clock. Paradise." Those three words turned the terror of the Bolshevik army into the blissful passivity of a puppy dog. A spell that would last long enough for Anna to get away, and for us to prepare for an experiment in morality that none of us ever dreamed about, with stakes far higher than we ever imagined.

Reel 8

"Shhh!!!" Tasha screamed at Nicholi as he set up the small stools in the attic of the Miller's Cottage. "They're coming."

"They're still three hundred yards away," Nicholi growled back. "Look at Anna. She has his ear, we will have his balls. Unless she wants to drain them out dry, ey?"

None of us had ever seen a jury before. Russian courts always dispensed guilty verdicts to Ukrainians, and Ukrainians always dealt with transgression by deferring them to higher authorities. The guilty punished themselves, so we thought. Or so the innocent among us believed.

There wasn't enough room for twelve people in the attic, so we decided on six jurors, like the Old West towns in Canada.

Johan was the judge. He would have whined about being judge between now and Judgment Day, and probably beyond, if we didn't give him the job. Besides, he liked being procedural, and we hated it. He could break a tie if there was one. Johan liked that kind of power.

Nicholi was the "head" juror. Our philosopher-king would not let us use his courtroom if we didn't give him some title of importance. But Nicholi knew Anna, and he knew Russians. He could smell a Russian lie a mile away. "Something in the breath," he claimed so many times, "Like rancid garlic. Only out of the mouth of a Russian do lies smell that foul." Of course, Nicholi was good at exaggerating the truth, and lied to himself on many occasions. But he was the most honest liar I ever met.

Next to Nicholi, Father Dimitri. For the purposes of jury discussion, we could call him Dimitri. He didn't like that rule much, but it was live with that rule or let Nicholi have his vote, and Father Dimitri would sooner hand over his pulpit to the devil himself.

Then there was Tasha. The only women who intervened in the legal affairs of men were gypsies or witches. Or women who used their most powerful weapon. "If women are not worthy to be on the jury, they are not worthy of being with their husbands on cold winter nights," Tasha pointed out. The threat of a strike by all women against all men in Telenkov was unthinkable, but Tasha's eyes were firm and determined. She was widowed, divorced from a husband we never knew, who left her for reasons she never spoke of. She also had far more influence on the women in Telenkov than any man. I never really knew why.

But one woman would be outnumbered by five men. Tasha insisted on another woman on the jury, citing evidence that even the Soviets were smart enough to value the council and power of a woman in civil affairs. Elena spoke softly and not very often. Her words were non-confrontational, except when she was told by her husband Sergei to verify a claim he loudly boasted. "Yes," "no," "Sergei knows what he is talking about," were the words that passed Elena's lips more than any others in public.

But what Elena would DO when something IMPORTANT came around, that was something else. She DID hide the village horses so they wouldn't be used for meat, and she did pay off his creditors after he publicly vowed to pay off the devil himself first. Pride is all that the nearly bankrupt farmer, blacksmith, potter, and carpenter had left. Sergei had less money than anyone in Telenkov, but Elena never let him feel like a poor man. She was the kind of person who needed to be needed.

Then there was me, the sixth juror. I really hadn't been to the Miller's Cottage before, though I boasted about how many times I became "experienced" there when I was a young man. I always wondered why women who are not sexually-experienced are called virgins, and why we are just called "inexperienced."

When I was a boy, I thought a lot about sex. Only men got to have sex. When I was a man, I would find out the secret of my gender.

I did get initiated into manhood, with a woman whose face I will always remember, but whose name I have long forgotten. I found it confusing. Something I sought and feared, both at the same time. Was I scared of intimacy? Was I beyond it? Did I have the unspeakable sexual orientation which did not involve animals? Was I born to be a scholar, priest or politician? I had heard that all three of these creatures were married to their work, and to the obsession of seeing God face to face, rather than feel His warm light on the back of a bent neck.

I wondered about such things. I also wondered what it would be like to see Anna naked, even while engaged and madly in love with Lorena, my first wife, who died a month before we were to bring our first child into the world. In a strange way, my lust for Anna made me love Lorena even more. I still don't know why. Truth be told, if cholera hadn't destroyed our marriage, we would have. At the altar ,me and Lorena knew it wouldn't work. But we went through the ceremony and the ritual of living as husband

and wife. Our families expected it. Besides, we were both already twenty-five and too afraid of facing life alone, or without the blessing of our families.

"Order! Come to order!" Johan said, slipping into his native Polish. As judge, he had the right to the gavel, Sergei's old blacksmith mallet. He was also the keeper of the books.

They included Father Dimitri's Bible, with pagemarkers pasted into the Old Testament. I never liked the Book of Deuteronomy. The hundreds of rules the Hebrews had to obey to be free in Jehovah's eyes. I always felt that TEN commandments were hard enough to follow.

Nadia said that Christians were lucky. Jesus told us to obey just one rule - to love each other. Still, Father Dimitri insisted on using the Hebrew laws of the Old Testament.

I once asked Father Dimitri, "Why insist that Jewish laws be used against Russian transgressors?"

True to form, he answered without missing a breath. "Because Jews are Pagans. Jewish law is Pagan law. Russians are Pagans. Therefore, we will judge them by Pagan laws. Punishment for their not being forgiven by Christ. Jewish law is the most merciful of Pagan law. As Christians, we must be merciful; therefore, we will use

Jewish law to judge the severity of offenses committed by the Pagan Russian sinners, therefore we can send them to Hell in a merciful, Christian manner."

Father Dimitri always used a lot of "therefores" to justify his own logic. If you let yourself slip away from your world and drift into his, he could convince you that the sky actually was green, and goad you into asking what shade of green it was.

Fortunately, there were two more legal books to use in our improvised courtroom. Behind the record of baptismal certificates and marriage records at the desk in the tavern we used to call city hall, there was the Holy Book of Ukrainian Ordinances. The pages were blurred by rain, wind, and sun, the letters bleached almost beyond readability. The fifth chapter, the largest, was devoted to the punishment of women who attempted sorcery. The sixth detailed punitive actions to be taken against witches who had successfully executed their spells.

A third book was to be used to break a legalistic tie. Johan brought it, of course. It was a Polish law book written in Johan's native tongue. Only Johan could understand it, of course. But only we could understand the Ukrainian Law Text, those of us who could read, that is.

But no matter what was in the books, we'd argue anyway. Still, we had to make our murder trials look legal, for ourselves and, perhaps, for God.

Three hundred yards is not a long distance to walk, but Anna took small steps, Lieutenant Reminkol holding her arm under his like he was strolling down the town square, protecting her from common thieves and beggars. Reminkol's eyes were smug. Anna's were nervous. She stopped at the door, her hand juggling the key.

"Are you nervous?" Reminkol commented to her in a voice that sounded ominously Germanic.

"I just never entertained someone as... important as you before," Anna related.

Reminkol smiled from the left side of his mouth. He took a puff on his cigarette. He gently took Anna's hand and kissed it.

Anna had never been kissed that way before, not by a Russian, Ukrainian, or even the Gypsy pimps. There was a strange kind of warmth to it, somehow. A warmth shared in a very private moment, Anna thought.

"Cigarette?" Reminkol said, offering Anna a puff.

Anna loved tobacco, and had not had a fresh cigarette since the November deep freeze. It was also her favorite brand, though on a minus-20-degree day, ANY tobacco would have been.

"Thank you," she said. She took a puff, warming her cold lungs with the fumes. An inhale, then an exhale. Then another.

Reminkol reached for the keys. "Allow me," he said.

Reminkol was not a patient man, with people, machinery, or the Ukrainian winter. Two failed turns of the key against a jammed lock was enough. Before Anna could blink her frozen eyelids, he whipped out his revolver. Five shots went into the lock, the first to open it, the next four to extract vengeance.

We shuddered in fear. Anna's breath stopped. Reminkol clicked his heels and allowed Anna first entry.

"I'll send a detail around to fix the lock tomorrow," he said. He was arrogant, calculating, and as aristocratic as any officer we had ever seen. But there was a kindness behind his steel eyes. It was that kindness that scared us most. What secret was he hiding? What would happen to us if we didn't find out fast enough?

CHAPTER 7

Boris was silent. It was a deafening silence, even to Geoff. He had heard that deafening silence only twice before. Once was at his thesis defense, after a barrage of questions that stumped him. Professor Brunowski pushed the young graduate student to the limit of any mortal's knowledge. The correct answer to the final set of inquiries was, "I don't know." Those words were not in Geoff's vocabulary, but the lone scholar in the future Dr. Weinburg's thesis committee insisted on him uttering them. "I don't know" was a common phrase spoken by a seasoned scientist like Brunowski. They resurrected primal fear in an arrogant one like Weinburg.

The second time silence drove terror into Geoff was during a home pregnancy test. The ever seductive, but very Catholic, Christine Berganti was not about to get an abortion. Geoff was equally reluctant to get married, despite Christine's close ties with her construction business family across the river in Jersey.

"It gets scarier from here on. From the inside and the outside," Yakov related.

Yakov seldom waxed philosophical. He was a realist. A realist that did not bullshit anyone, even himself.

Geoff's cellular rang. Strange, since it had been out of order ever since he landed in Leningrad.

"God calling?" Geoff said jokingly.

"Probably," Yakov replied.

"Better to listen to the stories of PEOPLE first," Boris added.

Geoff let the phone ring. He didn't know why. The rules of this game were changing every time he figured them out, and the consequences were getting more severe with each word the Ukrainian madman uttered.

Questions rumbled through Geoff's head. Why had he been given top secret clearance by the U. S. State Department, but nothing from the Soviet side? Why was every letter Yakov mailed across the Atlantic to him steamed open first? Why were very official-looking green cars pulling up to strategic parking spots outside the complex, passengers and drivers hidden inside, faces and agendas very hidden?

"Ignorant people are happy people," Yakov said. "I think Cervantes said that. Maybe it was Bob Dylan. Maybe Einstein."

Geoff loved to gamble, but only if he knew he could win the game, or had nothing to lose.

"I was happy, once. It was the most miserable two weeks of my life," Geoff replied. His words were clever. His fear was real. His new Russian and Ukrainian comrades appreciated his courage.

The phone rang on, then stopped. Boris spoke.

Reel 9

Anna was never scared, so I heard. Whores were always in control, the only ones who could direct their spontaneous passion. They were the Angels who God secretly sent to Earth to give us love of life when religion made us too obsessed with death.

I always thought that God, if He did exist, was more alive than Holy. In my more lucid moments, I secretly thought that He wanted to be found out. To have someone uncover his bag of tricks so we could appreciate his humanity.

"God must be a very lonely person. Up there in the sky with no one to laugh with," I once commented to Father Dimitri. "Why does God never smile?" It was one of the only questions Father Dimitri never answered.

Anna always seemed more powerful than God or Father Dimitri. Maybe it was her eyes. Sometimes they were deep blue, like the limitless sky. Sometimes brown, inviting you in from the cold. Sometimes silver. Sometimes hazel. It was a trick that worked on all of us. It would NOT work on Lieutenant Reminkol.

Reminkol had too much experience with whores, from London to Siberia, to be taken in by the tricks of a working class gypsy like Anna. He could see what Anna was thinking. She couldn't lie to him and get away with it. He knew it. She knew it. And we knew it.

Why Reminkol came into the Miller's Cottage that day, I will never know. He must have seen that Anna was up to something sinister. I think that Reminkol took it as a challenge.

Reminkol looked around at the velvet curtains covering the windows, then the satin linen covering the bed. On the walls, paintings. One by REAL artists. The kind who got paid in money instead of chickens. Murals that glorified the pleasures of the flesh, instead of the persecution of the spirit.

Anna lit a candle mounted in a gold stand that somehow had avoided being confiscated. She poured century-old Napoleon brandy into two snifters. They were special snifters - stolen by her father from Czar Nicholas while he was still drinking from them, the stories went. She offered a brandy to Reminkol, along with a warm smile. Neither was accepted.

"Interesting room," Reminkol said. "Interesting decorations." He smiled. It was a familiar smile. The one the Russians used just before they took our food, homes, and dignity.

He walked around the room, three times, one hand behind his back, the other on the handle of his revolver. He had read many American Western novels, we heard, and enjoyed the quick-draw. He also enjoyed the kill. The scores of bodies lying dead in the snow outside Basilova attested to that. So the stories went.

There were lots of stories about Reminkol's cruelty. No one had the courage to ask how many of them were really true. Those who did wound up dead. It was up to us to find out if that was because Reminkol was really the worst butcher in the Soviet Union, or the most effective and desperate bluffer.

We could have jumped him, but one of us would have been shot, killed or, worse, maimed. A price too high for ANY victory. Maybe that was why the Russians had the guns and we had the terror.

We watched Reminkol from our observation chairs in the attic. Father Dimitri crossed himself and said the fastest prayer he could remember. Nicholi froze in his boots. Johan held his breath in his throat. Elena shook. Her husband, Sergei, gave her a reassuring hug, urine trickling down his trousers.

What I remember most clearly is Anna, her lips quivering around a smile that took all the courage in the world to keep. Maybe I helped give her that courage. Men like to think such things, particularly Telenkov men.

Reminkol turned around. The smile on his face widened. He whipped out his knife, its tip sharp as a serpent's tongue. He held it to Anna's chest, popping the buttons off, one at a time.
With the third, a look at Anna's body, and a smile of approval.

He cordially picked up the brandy glasses and handed Anna one of them. He bowed slightly. "I'm used to being in control. I'm sure you understand." Then, the kind of respect a professional military man gives a professional lady.

Anna took a sip of brandy, though she felt like pouring the entire bottle down her breathless throat. Reminkol gulped down his, then hurled the glass against the wall behind him like a drunken Greek sailor. He grinned, then went for the top button on his shirt.

"No, let me," Anna interrupted. The chest of a man is always the most sensitive spot, particularly on a braggart. It was a reliable place to start.

Anna snuck her hands inside Reminkol's shirt, rubbing him, working her way up to his neck, then below his waist. He closed his eyes, hypnotized with pleasure. Reminkol was the kind of man who liked to be both seduced and served. The kind who would want a woman to strip him down. And the kind of man who would take off his gun last, if at all.

Anna led Reminkol to bed. He followed, stripped of his uniform, but not his control. He kept his gun around his waist, but between his thighs, the third leg was growing stiffer and, it seemed, longer with every stroke Anna delivered around his neck. She caressed his body, inch by inch, breaking him down, slowly. Slow was the only way to reach the boy inside a man like Reminkol, and slow took a long time.

Again, we watched. Elena was curious and disappointed with Reminkol's anatomy, and perhaps secretly admiring Anna's. Women know love better than men ever will, and God knows that Elena had not had a man who could give her all the love she needed. Sergei tried, but you can't ask a land-bound bear to join you on a trip to the store.

Sergei was embarrassed. It was surprising to me. He always told the dirtiest jokes in town.

Nicholi sneered. "When Reminkol confesses what he did to Anna, I get to cut his penis off. And roast it. I want to stick it in his mouth, and show off his head to ANYone who runs the kind of prison camps he was in charge of. I'll offer Anna that bastard's testicles, but I'll have his head." Nicholi spoke softly, but with a different kind of anger. The kind of anger that had fear underneath it.

Father Dimitri stroked his beard. He never trimmed his beard much. He said it was a priest's holy obligation to have a beard. He said it was to appear more holy to God and to us. But all of us knew that he hid behind it. Some secret that involved Anna, maybe. His whiskers couldn't hide his sorrowful eyes, and his jealous heart.

In Johan's eyes, wonderment. He had, so he told us, traveled around the world as an investment banker. He had, so he told us, dined with Kings, Kaisers, and even American Congressmen. But though he held more university degrees than there were universities in Ukraine, Johan was inexperienced in life. He always kept his distance. From us. And from Anna. Maybe that was why he was looking at her so intensely. Like a lover. A friend. A mother. After all, Anna could be all three at once, and still know how to let a man keep his dignity.

I was as helpless as anyone else in the attic. I knew that we had to do it this way. That we needed a REAL confession from Reminkol. We needed to find out if he really was the butcher everyone said he was. It would ease our consciences. We also needed to know what the plans were for Telenkov. If anyone knew what was in store for us according to Comrade Stalin's always-changing Five-Year plan, it was Reminkol.

But using Anna? It felt like a betrayal. Like cowardice. Like I was sending a sister, lover, or wife in front of me to look for land mines. It was a man's job to protect a woman, and it was Anna who was protecting us.

Finally, Reminkol made his move. After he had had his fill of gentle strokes, he flipped Anna on her back. She offered no resistance. Reminkol always needed to be on top. It was the only way he felt at ease, and did he ever feel at ease. His groans turned into screams of hunger, then fear, then ecstasy. Then relief, as his semen flowed into Anna's vagina.

It took Reminkol a long time to release his defective sperm into Anna's always perfect body. There was a lot on his mind, Anna must have been thinking. And a lot he would tell, now that Anna had gotten the better part of him.

Anna kissed him, under his jaw, then on his forehead. His body went limp, all resistance and fight gone. Anna released the buckle on his holster belt. Reminkol hardly noticed, or did not care.

It was Anna's turn to be in control, Reminkol's turn to talk. And our turn to listen.

"Tell me about your mother, your father, your family," Anna said tenderly, as Reminkol nestled his head between her bosoms.

Reminkol smiled, then spoke in a voice more froglike than human, and more childlike than manly. "You don't want to know."

"I do," Anna said. It was so convincing that even I believed it. "You're a special man. I'm interested in special men. Where did this special man in my arms grow up?"

Reminkol squeezed Anna's hand. She brought him closer to her bosom, trying to keep him from coming too close to her heart.

"Tell me about your father. Your mother. Do you have any brothers? Were you ever married? Did you ever have a child? A horse? A dog?"

Reminkol's denial turned into fond remembrance. "Ivan. I called him Ivan. Ivan the Terrible."

"Tell me about Ivan. What kind of dog was he?"

Again, silence, then a flood of tears waiting to come out of Reminkol's hard eyes. "I found him on my father's farm. Raised him from a pup. I kept him. He was good company. My best friend."

Anna knew that Ivan was Reminkol's ONLY friend. She hugged him. He held on to her arm like it was a limb, keeping him from falling into an abyss of grief he could never crawl out of.

Anna told a story. She was good at telling people what she was thinking through stories. "I had a cat. Katerini. A stupid-looking cat. With three legs. I never thought a cat would live with three legs, but..."

Reminkol was crying, but only on the inside. As hard as anyone I'd ever seen. "I wanted to be an artist," he bellowed in a meek voice choked at the throat. "I was a good artist. The best sculptor in my town. There was a wild horse in the woods. All white. No one could catch the horse with a rope, but I could catch its spirit - in stone. I worked for months. My father bought me the best tools, the best clay. But he said I'd pay a high price for them, one day. I spent all summer and fall watching the horse, then shaped its likeness in clay. Then finally, Christmas came. Siegfried was ready. A horse with spirit. Passion."

He hadn't told this story for a long time. Anna stroked his face, tenderly. A tear trickled down his cheek, but a small one, the floodgates still closed.

"I rode Siegfried into town on my parent's anniversary. Pulled on a sled. I paid the chimney-sweep to pull me into the town square. The horse was too heavy for me to drag myself and I was going to prove to EVERYone that I could make something real. Something beautiful. I wasn't just a spoiled noble's son who could do nothing except look important."

"I heard cheers. Screams. 'Hail General Reminkol!!! Hail General Reminkol.' I raised my head, high. The first time I raised my head high in town. I saw the sky. Big, bold sky. Then from out of it..."

Anna knew what Reminkol was thinking. She made him say it. For his sake and ours. "Buckets of manure and urine!!! They were waiting for me to come and laugh at me. All of them!!! The boys I went to school with. The servants. Mother. And father. I fell off the horse. The head cracked. My father laughed hardest then. As the piss and shit froze on my face, I swore I'd..."

Reminkol's steel-blue eyes turned beet-red. I never saw a Russian look more human. More real. More like us. Even the ever-vengeful Nicholi had compassion in his eyes. This was someone else who could barely kill a mouse. Maybe someone who was bluffing his way up the Kremlin political ladder.

Anna moved in closer to Reminkol. A desperate Russian with a gun strapped to his waist was dangerous, no matter how shaky his hand was.

Anna's instincts about a man's pain were seldom wrong. Her knowledge about a man's anger was not always so good.

Reminkol grabbed his gun, his grief and pain absorbed into rage. "NO one is going to laugh at me again!!! They stopped laughing at me in Vasilevka. In Drenkov. In Star Golesk.
And Barvenkova."

"Barvenkova," Nicholi muttered under his breath. Again, and again. I was the only one who could see it, I think. I dared not say anything.

Reminkol screamed, shooting bullets into the walls. He must have killed those ghosts ten thousand times, but they were more alive than ever. "They fear my name, now. I don't have to do ANYthing and they fear my name. I'm laughing at them now. I'm laughing at THEM!!!"

Reminkol had eight bullets in his gun, I think. He only had the chance to fire off four. Nicholi jumped him. "Barvenkova! Barvenkova!" Nicholi screamed, his hands grabbing Reminkol's throat so tightly that I could hear the bones break. Before we could get down to help Nicholi carry out what was now a guilty verdict forced upon all of us, it was finished. Reminkol's face was pale white, his body shaking like a chicken after its head was chopped off.

"Why?" Father Dimitri asked Nicholi. "You're becoming worse than they are. We have to use our brains, our minds, our hearts. Be more clever than they are. He could have told us what the Russians are going to do with us. If they want us alive or dead."

"Barvenkova!" Nicholi repeated again. and again. With that, he took out his knife and cut off Reminkol's testicles, then his scalp, with the skill of a surgeon, a professional job completed in less than ten seconds. It seemed that Nicholi had been practicing the procedures in his sleep ever since he came back from the war he never talked about.

Nicholi put Reminkol's coat on Anna, gently hugged her, and left. "The Russians kill you slowly. So it hurts more," he told us again.

Nicholi walked slowly into the woods, one very big step closer to death. We should have expected it. There was a lot of hurt in Nicholi. He didn't know how to be clever, to manipulate people, or get around them. The only alternative to surrendering his dignity was to fight. He had the right to survive the only way he knew how. We admired him and chastised him. And shared the fruits of his kill in the absence of his company.

Reel 9

We ate well that night. Very well. Fresh-killed Bolshevik was very tasty. Especially with some garlic to add some spice to their dried-out souls. No Easter leg of lamb tasted more succulent. No spring chicken is more juicy. We all had a taste of it in the Miller's Cottage. Each of us would take what was left to the rest of the people in the village.

We had a drop-off system, something we became very good at. It was the first thing we felt good about in a long time. "Russian Delight!" Sergei said, as he rolled up his meat delivery in the Ukrainian version of Pravda, which we were encouraged to read as part of our political education. "After this is over, Elena and I are going into the restaurant business. Lenin-perogies. Stalin-sausage links. Make a killing off of all the tourists from Moscow, Or a killing WITH them."

His laughter was contagious, and I found myself joining in. Even Father Dimitri chuckled. It was the first time I heard him chuckle. Johan, of course, was the last to join in. He never really shared our sense of humor. But he did share our poverty - and pathos - despite the fact that he kept trying to convince himself that he was more aristocratic than us, in a democratic way, of course.

Elena smiled, but didn't laugh. It was a sad smile, a very sad one. True, it was a long time since there was something important Sergei could control, and he was entitled. Maybe Elena had smelled hot air behind Reminkol's boasts of cruelty. Maybe she pitied the hurt boy inside Reminkol, instead of hating the man he had become.

Sympathy is easy for women. Hating is easier for men. So it seemed.

Anna looked at Elena. "The children have to eat. They need us to be alive for them." That's what it was all about. Even Tasha agreed, laying aside her anger and ultimate revenge on Anna for another day.

Maybe Anna's love for children came from her never being able to have any. Tar had been poured into her vagina in Hungary, so I heard from Nadia. It was during the war. Nadia didn't tell me whether it was the Germans, the Russians, the British, the French, or the American Expedition. It was a squad of soldiers. A small band of ordinary men turned into a vicious pack. The thrill of conquest offered by the devil to six boys with lonely, boring lives in peacetime, who would selectively remember what they wanted to about a brief-lived manhood during the war.

Nadia told me about it at Anna's request. Anna wanted someone "respectable" in Telenkov to know. Someone she could trust. It meant a lot that Anna trusted me. It meant a lot more to her that I didn't betray that trust.

The next day, we showed up for work on schedule. When Reminkol didn't appear for his noon inspection at the usual mid-morning hour, the Russian enlisted men cheered. Our spirits were more somber, but our bodies would not let us escape the wrath of how we did what we had to do the night before.

An empty stomach fed very quickly hurts. We ALL hurt. When we were summoned to do road work by the Russian officers who were left, I could barely move my shovel. Sergei was doubled over. I remembered that there's an organ near the stomach, the pancreas. If starving wolves got into the butcher's backroom, they got sick and almost died. "Pancreatitis," Ivan the butcher would say when he caught the dying wolves in the woods. That, or "botulism." They were the only two medical words he knew, and he used them a lot. Then, of course, he'd shoot the wolf.

The only cure I knew for pancreatitis or botulism was compassion, warmth, and prayer. The Russians would soon get around to figuring out where Reminkol was, but there was enough time for that in the afternoon.

Father Dimitri and me dragged Sergei back home. I could barely stand up myself, and Father Dimitri vomited out a green trail on top of the wind-frozen snow.

"God, thank you for this pain," Father Dimitri said. "Thank you for giving us this pain." He was sincere. More sincere than I ever thought he could be. And insightful. True, we looked for pain wherever we could find it, so that we could atone for any pleasures that found their way to us on earth. No man - or woman-could get into heaven after a life where there was more pleasure than pain.

But there was wisdom in what Dimitri kept groaning under his frozen breath. God, or whoever was in charge of the madness which we were experiencing here on earth, had reminded us to keep us from getting too crazy. Too evil. Too much like the Bolsheviks we were fighting against. So we hoped.

We would never know if Reminkol was as cruel as he said he was. Did we kill the devil, or one of his victims who was lured into evil by blind hatred? We agonized a lot. We were very good at agonizing. The Russians weren't.

A new arrival, Captain Denesovic came up to me. Two men were behind him, cold, hard looks on their clean-shaven faces. With Reminkol gone, Denesovic could take control of Telenkov, and us. "You," he said to me. "The Major wants to see you."

Father Dimitri was given permission to take Sergei home. A jack of all trades in Telenkov was a master of most of them in Moscow, and Sergei's survival was ensured as long as he got back to work in the afternoon.

Denesovic wasn't concerned about the two missing Russian officers. He was Lithuanian. But he was still a

Bolshevik Lithuanian. He'd get around to looking into why two of the most hated officers in Telenkov disappeared without a trace. If the enlisted men killed Captain Korsikov and Lieutenant Reminkol, they would get an invisible medal from Denesovic and the best bottle of vodka he could confiscate. He even seemed proud of us for what we had done to and with Korsikov and Reminkol. Or what he may have surmised that we did.

A trick I could use one day, I thought. Make the Russians suspicious of each other. I was not very good at being clever, but I tried anyway.

As I was marched up the street, I tried to think more quietly. "The Russians can hear you think," Nicholi told us. Or was it Nadia who said that?

"Move!" I heard behind me, a rifle stuck into my back. When the Russians stuck a rifle in your back, they were really mad like they knew something. Like they knew you were guilty of something.

I was more frightened of what was ahead of me than behind me. From the Major's room on the third floor of his headquarters, music. Beethoven, again. The Opus 110 for violin and piano. It was my favorite. Half a duet, played on a new piano. All that was needed was a violin.

We hadn't seen the Major for weeks. But traffic went in and out of his office. The civilians I saw go in never came out, especially the ones who were blindfolded.

I was too terrified to be scared when the soldiers put a urine-stained rag over my eyes and led me upstairs. They say life flashes before your eyes at the last hour. I had seen flashes before, but not as brightly as then. And not so confused. Death was supposed to be more firm than this, I thought. It was panic. Internal chaos.

The staircase wound upward on more steps than I thought possible in a three-story building. I wondered if I really believed in God. "I think I do," my heart told my mind. But it wasn't God I was concerned about, it was still the people what I had done to them, or for them. And how bravely I could face what was to come. "God has to honor bravery and humanity," I thought, an atheist's prayer that never failed me. The Beethoven sustained me, too. I sang along with the piano, filling in violin passages in my head as well as I could remember them.

I was left at the top of the stairs. The soldiers went downstairs. The music stopped. I kept singing. Suddenly, a bright flash of light appeared in my eyes. In front of me, the Major. Smiling. A kind smile. A bright room.

He asked me in, then bolted the door behind him. His eyes were something I would never forget. Bluer and bigger than I ever saw. Like there was an infinity in the sky inside them. He spoke to me in notes. Singing them, then playing them on the piano.

A violin was laid on the table. Next to it, a biscuit, a glass of tea, and a piece of meat. Meat spiced with garlic and basil. How and why a delivery of "Reminkol Delight" got to the Major, I do not know. Why he didn't care, I was afraid to ask.

Strangely, there was only the music. Music that drew me into the Major's inner world. An inner world I wanted to enter since before I could dream.

I let the bow glide along the strings as I merged with the adagio movement. Then the fortissimo, fast and hard. Then the third movement, laughter coming out of every note. We roared out while playing. Roared out louder laughter than I could remember.

I don't know how long we played, or how many of the sonatas we shared. There was one I liked. Opus 135, as I remember. The last one. The one Beethoven must have written as he was passing over to Paradise. I started it, my soul soaring higher than Heaven itself. From the Major - silence. A grave silence.

"Not now. Not yet," he said. They were the only words he spoke. By way of explanation, he played Bach. Bach was safe, simple. Something you could appreciate without diving deep into the depths of your soul.

Beethoven would be played tomorrow, I thought. We would finish today with Bach.

We ate, not exchanging a word. "Silence after beautiful music is good," I could hear him say behind his kind, but very troubled eyes.

"Tomorrow, ten o'clock?" he asked me.

A Ukrainian slave being ASKED? With such respect? I was touched. Honored. I always wanted to do an important thing for important people. Everyone in Telenkov was important to me. But so was the Major.

"Tomorrow. Ten o'clock," I said.

I bowed my head slightly, out of respect. The Major bowed at the waist, out of friendship.

He went back to his post at the window, staring out at the setting sun, losing himself in the infinity beyond the flaming-red horizon. One day I'd join him there, I thought - and feared.

I opened the door. Behind it, Russian soldiers, ready to escort me home. "Tomorrow. Ten o'clock," I said to them in Russian, showing enough confidence to regain my own dignity, but not enough pride to get me killed. It was only the beginning of a contest of wills and insights that I could not afford to lose.

CHAPTER 8

"Professor Rostilski, please let us in," the man screamed into the megaphone from outside what to Geoff seemed more like a bunker than an interview room in an abandoned sanitorium. "Yakov," he repeated, after being ignored for twenty seconds that seemed like an hour. The voice was booming, and deep.

"It's Hartunian," Yakov said to Geoff. "My old mentor. The smartest biochemist I know, still."

"Almost-Nobel Laureate, three years in a row. At least twenty publications a year between 1965 and 1987," Geoff recalled. "I didn't know he was still alive."

"He isn't. He went into administration."

"Better to be a hammer than a nail, Yakov."

"Better to be published than to be right. Medical fairy tales based in imaginary facts are, as we know..." Yakov hesitated.

"Hartunian? Faking data?" Geoff gasped. He invented modern lipid chemistry."

"In his own image," Yakov replied. He was silent. Hurt. Betrayed.

"Why didn't you call him out? If he committed the big no-no, he has to be called out." Geoff asserted. "I'm an asshole, but I never cheated. We both stole ideas, but never made up wrong ones. Not on purpose."

Yakov was still silent. Professor, now Science Minister, Hartunian wasn't.

"Doctor Weinburg. May we talk to YOU?" Hartunian sounded very human. Remorseful, but still dangerous.

Geoff's cellular rang. Five, six, ten times. He picked it up.

"Weinburg," Geoff answered.

"We want the prisoner," Hartunian said calmly.

"I was brought here to observe a patient, not a prisoner."

"You were brought here to study an index case for an epidemic disease."

"How isolated?"

Hartunian hesitated.

"What disease?" Geoff pressed.

Hartunian was quiet. Tanks emerged on the horizon, ones with real rounds in their guns. Geoff hadn't even seen tanks or what they could do. Yakov had.

"If you fire those guns, you'll NEVER get what you came for," Yakov yelled into the phone.

"Yakov. You have as much to lose as we do. Please, let us have the prisoner. For his sake, and ours." Hartunian's tone was reasonable, calm and rational. Yakov's reply wasn't.

"Fuck off and die, you motherfucking asshole!!! Fuck yourself up the ass and screw your own brains out." Yakov's English lacked accuracy, but the meaning was clear enough. Hartunian yelled back some Russian insults vulgar enough to make even Geoff cringe, then hung up. Yakov clenched his fist, defiantly and with a healthy measure of self-confidence.

Yakov knew it would come to this, and was well prepared. A force field shielded the interrogation complex like a wild mother bison around a newborn calf. Bullets couldn't penetrate without being deflected, and anything biological entering the protected zone would be burned to a crisp in two seconds flat.

Yakov had rewired and embellished the security well against intruders. It was ironic, the best trained biophysicist in Moscow using all that training against a system that gave him everything he ever had. The biomagnetic laser system could hold up against anything. As long as the invaders couldn't find the emergency batteries, one uncertain variable. And as long as the batteries could hold out, another very uncertain variable.

"What do they want, Yakov?!!" Geoff asked as the tanks surrounded the complex, like vultures on dying prey.

"Whatever it is, we can't give it to them," Yakov replied.

"Why?" Geoff countered. "If I'm gonna die in a Soviet Alamo, I have the right to know why."

"Every day for us here is our last stand at the Alamo," Yakov replied.

Yakov took out another tape and put it on the machine. He flipped a coin in the air.

"Our last publication, Dr. Weinburg. Heads, I get first authorship. Tails, you get top billing."

The coin hit the ground. The tanks fired a warning round across the roof. Boris picked up the coin. He smirked, bit into it, and continued.

Reel 10

My days belonged to the Major, the nights to my Ukrainian comrades. There was not much time left for me, but maybe I wanted it that way.

Our business at the Miller's Cottage, which doubled as a courtroom and kitchen, had to be conducted at night. Captain Denesovic strictly carried out the Major's orders about fraternization with local women within town limits. They were the only ones that were.

Everything else was carried out according to Moscow's timetable, and Denesovic was as ignorant of that timetable as we were. Still, Denesovic could justify our existence as "Necessary Indigenous Personnel" - for a while.

It was Sergei who bought us some time as January blew in. Give Sergei ten thousand rubles in the morning, and he'd be fifty rubles in debt by nightfall. Johan earned half his living off of Sergei, taking no blame for his God-given talent for ignoring good investments and indulging in bad ones.

"Better to spend your last ruble on an investment than on food," Sergei kept saying to Elena, or anyone else who was within the sound of his booming voice. "God rewards those who are persistent."

This time, he was right. There was still some "Reminkol Delight" left, enough for Elena to re-cook, and garnish with herb stubs she managed to pull out of the ground before the few remaining field mice got to them. Denesovic loved chicken, the only thing he really missed from home, 1,500 miles over the Northern horizon and a lifetime away.

Denesovic came to the door, letting himself in. He kept asking Sergei if he could meet the cook who could stimulate his cultured palate in such a non-cultured place. Though a skilled soldier and a born administrator, Denesovic's passion was in the kitchen. He dreamed of being a great chef. "I could prepare the food, but never give life to it. A gift I would give my right hand for," he confessed. "If I could make chicken like this, Master Cook, just once, I would die an ecstatic man."

Sergei told Denesovic that he had to keep the cook's identity secret. If his identity was known to anyone except the "squire" charged with looking after him, the Spirits would steal his culinary skills AND his ability to coax 'wild chickens' out of the bush and into the pot.

Denesovic seemed to believe the story. Sergei became so good at embellishing the fairy tale that he started to believe it himself. But even Sergei's ability to tell stories and Elena's skill as a cook couldn't create chicken for Denesovic's dining table indefinitely. We needed fresh meat, something in scarce supply for us AND the Russians.

There was no way that Elena could make something that tasted close to "Reminkol Delight" with anything but human meat. Even if we DID get hold of corpses that passed through town on the trucks, they were rotted. Our lives depended on replicating the recipe that Reminkol forfeited his life to give us.

"It's the way you kill them, not cook them," Nicholi said, as we huddled in the attic of the Miller's Cottage, waiting for Anna's next client. "When they're terrified, it makes the meat taste fresher. Gamier. Like you're getting nutrition from your prey's body AND soul."

We had to invite Denosevic to stay whenever he decided to treat us to a friendly visit.. True, he believed that the only Russians not worthy of death by hanging were one-month old babies. But though he wore a Red Army uniform with as much pride as any other officer, he was one of us. And if he wasn't, we had to let him think he still was. Who knows what Denosivic would do in a blind rage if we rejected him? But Denosevic did know Russians, and could smell through a lie better than any of us. So, why did he continue to let us lie to him? And what did he want for his silence regarding what we had done, and continued to do? In any case,Denosevic bid us all a good night and went on his way back to his quarters.

"So, where is the next customer?" Tasha blurted out when Denosevic was our of hearing range. "The slut said he would be here by now."

"Her name is Anna," Elena reminded Tasha.

Had the reminder come from a man, Tasha would have provided the Russians with a corpse of our own.

Hatred among women is far more vicious than between men. No rules to it, no boundaries. At least that was the way I saw it. It frightened me. And fascinated me. It was one of the many private sins I confessed only to myself.

Finally, there was a knock at the door. Anna approached, her slinky body and succulent breasts wrapped in a floor-length muskox shawl, a string of bear claws around her neck. All according to the request of the client, Sergeant Romanoff, an artillery soldier who lost most of his hearing in the Great War, fighting the Kaiser. For valiant service to the Red Army in the Siberian campaign, he was awarded a gold medal that turned green two days later, and a hearing aid that never worked, though he tried to convince himself that it did. Romanoff was a bitter man, a forty-year-old Sergeant who hadn't had a promotion in over ten years, and knew life wouldn't get any better. He took it out on us on more than one occasion, when Denesovic wasn't looking.

Romanoff loved artillery and discipline, and he served both mistresses faithfully. He often strapped one member of a work detail across the barrel of a cannon. Failure to complete the road construction ahead of schedule would result in an "accident." Sometimes he used his own soldiers like that, too. "Motivation," he called it. That motivation got the roads built ahead of schedule and kept him alive.

Most of us had already decided Romanoff's fate. So did the non-Russian recruits suffering under Romanoff's command. To share "beef Romanoff" with those homesick conscripts was something we yearned for. But reaching out to a stranger who could be your closest friend was a very dangerous thing in those times. One in ten soldiers belonged to the Secret Police, a fact which we knew all too well.

Anna let the door knock a second, then a third time. "Anticipation is what a man really likes most," she said to me once. It was all too true. My anticipation of knowing Anna in the way most men knew her had been simmering for nearly a decade.

She opened the door. We gritted our teeth and sharpened our knives. We each silently argued with the other over what body part we would get to share with our families, and which hunks of flesh would be given, perhaps sold, back to the Russians as the mystery-chef's secret Ukrainian recipe.

We were becoming smart people. Tied to the ways of the world. Practical. Persistent. But still not clever enough.

A young recruit stood in the doorway. "I'm Basili. Basili Yelstin." His face was clean-shaven, a six-month-old peachfuzz mustache over his frozen lips. "Sergeant Romanoff won't be here till midnight. He sent me ahead. For my birthday present," he continued.

He swaggered in, then gave Anna his coat. He warmed his hands at the fire, then poured eight hearty gulps of Anna's vodka down his throat. There was an air of unchallenged authority to him, the arrogance of youth, fueled by dumb luck and liquor.

"What's your name? Your REAL name," Anna asked. She kept her distance. Nineteen year olds like this one wanted to make the first move. "I can make it better for you if I know your real name," she continued.

"Tristan," he confessed, in a milder tone, with an accent that was more Ukrainian than Russian. "My mother insisted on giving it to me. She didn't tell me what it meant. From some opera, I think. I never liked opera."

Tristan had second thoughts. A whore who could see so much about him so early could find out other secrets. Two minutes of pleasure with any woman was not worth a lifetime of misery in a labor camp.

"Maybe next year," Tristan said. "I get to have another birthday next year." It was a wish we all hoped for.

Anna buttoned up Tristan's coat. "It's cold outside. Don't want you getting consumption before your next birthday, in a month or two?"

Anna was wise to keep him wanting to come back. An eager customer is one you can trust or use. Besides, it felt wrong to keep Tristan there when he didn't want to be, and at that time, we still had a sense of right and wrong. Besides, Romanoff would be coming in two hours. We could keep ourselves occupied arguing about something in our hidden observation posts in the attic.

I glanced over at Nicholi. Thank God he had the good sense to trust Anna's instincts instead of his rage.

But there was one set of eyes I couldn't trust. "Tristan," Father Dimitri bellowed in a voice that echoed throughout the room. He repeated it three times, from a place inside him I never knew.

Tristan aimed his rifle at the attic and shot five, maybe ten rounds. He didn't know where the voices were coming from, but whoever was up there did not have his welfare in mind. Tristan was the kind of soldier who shot first and maybe asked questions later. Maybe that was why he was still alive.

We held our breaths. Miraculously, we were still alive. Elena thanked God for sparing the life of her husband and herself. Johan silently thanked Nicholi for wasting so much wood in building the attic floor. Father Dimitri stared down, absorbed in a world of his own. I could always read what emotions were going on behind Father Dimitri's eyes, but not then.

Father Dimitri glanced down at Anna. She could feel his penetrating stare on her back and looked up. Whatever it took to keep this young soldier here, Father Dimitri would do. Tristan was going to go through the trial, just like everyone else.

Three feet below us, Tristan reloaded. He let his gun barrel smell out the unseen intruder. Ukraine was just as scary for a lone, raw Russian recruit as it was for unarmed civilians, a fact we did not fully appreciate. But Anna did.

"Ghosts," she said to Tristan. "Spirits, really. They want you to be here. They want US to be here. Together." She eased his mind with a caress of his chest.

Anna's hands were warm. Tristan shivered. His face turned white, paler than any ghost. With his right hand firmly on the trigger, he swung his left arm around Anna. Another two echoing "Tristans" from the attic caused him to shake so much that the gun slipped out of his hand. Anna was the only reality he had left, and he clung to her.

We should have thought of it sooner. The Russians tried to make us believe Bolshevik propaganda, why not use Ukrainian propaganda against the Reds?

Two kinds of people can be duped by ghost stories, the evil and the innocent. Which one Tristan was would be decided according to procedure. Who was in charge of the proceedings was another matter.

Anna went about it the usual way. The backrub to ease Tristan's fear, the chest massage to make him trust her. But it seemed to be more than that.

Loners with intelligence have to read to stay sane, and Anna was the most lonely smart woman I ever met. She had been to India once, Nadia told me. She learned about points on a man's body that can be touched. Points that could make him see like an eagle or become as insane as a rabid dog. Or maybe it was a kind of energy Anna could transfer with her body. Anna read a lot of books about "energy," too. "Tantra," I think I heard Nadia call it.

Anna pulled Tristan's head to her breasts. He melted into her arms like a baby. Where his penis was, I did not know. Anna caressed his groin, perhaps to ease his fears, or perhaps to connect his soul to hers through a vaginal bridge. Father Dimitri's groans, moans, and growls did not make her job any easier.

She told Tristan that the ghosts only wanted to know what was in his heart. That they could protect him as long as he told the truth, whatever it was. The ghost in the attic was silent. Above all, Father Dimitri needed to know the truth about Tristan.

"Where are you from?" Anna asked.

"Leningrad. When it used to be Saint Petersburg," Tristan answered, relieved to hear only the howling winter wind above him.

"You have scars on your body. Where did you get this one?"

"Fighting the Czars' Cossacks in Minsk. When I was a boy."

"And this one?"

"Fighting Counter-Revolutionaries in Lithuania. When I became a man."

"And this one?"

A vulnerable silence from the brave soldier.

"The ghosts want to know," Anna informed Tristan. "They won't let you go till you tell them."

Father Dimitri let out an angry groan.

"My father. The second one. He came to live with us when I was twelve," Tristan confessed.

Father Dimitri was silent. A very loud silence. The five-inch slash across Tristan's chest went a lot deeper than a quarter-inch of skin. It had penetrated into his heart, and the wound was still bleeding.

"But I killed him," Tristan said. "My second father."

Anna let her head rest on Tristan's chest.

"Why did you kill him?" she asked.

"He said that I hit my mother. Caused her pain."

"Did you, hit your mother?"

"I had to. I had no choice."

"Why?"

"I was in Leningrad."

"And...?"

Tristan suddenly felt at ease. Confident and proud of what life had made him.

"She was a counter-revolutionary. And a whore. I had to teach her a lesson. I gave her a choice. I could beat her in front of my superior for being a whore, or turn her in as a counter-revolutionary spy."

"Did you enjoy it?"

"Yes. I think so." There was no remorse in Tristan's voice. Life had bred it out of him.

"Where is your mother now? Did you try to help her?" Anna asked.

"No, she helped ME. When I turned her in for giving out counter-revolutionary pamphlets, they gave me a medal and a promotion. Let me show it to you." Anna pretended to admire the medal Tristan proudly waved in front of her eyes.

"I got the honor of shooting her. Right here," Tristan continued, pointing to Anna's forehead, then kissing it.

The knife in Dimitri's heart went deep into his soul.

It was time for a vote. Nicholi put his thumb down first. Sergei, Elena, and Johan followed. Then Tasha's vote was affirmed by a nod of admiration for Anna's ingenuity. I put my thumb down, then up, then declined to vote. It was not my decision to make, nor one that could be decided by a jury.

"Father Dimitri?" I asked the priest who, for the first time, sought comfort in MY troubled soul.

"He deserves to die. My son deserves to die." Dimitri tore off his crucifix and wept. He handed Nicholi the knife.

"I'll make it fast. Painless," Nicholi said, with the sincerity of a brother and a friend.

"No!" Dimitri countered. "I want him to feel the pain. I want him to know WHERE he is going and WHY!"

Dimitri snuck out the back window. He left his coat and crucifix behind. The only thing he took with him was a knife.

Nicholi took care of Tristan. A rope, slowly twisted around the neck. A "ten minute special," Nicholi called it. The brain gets confused, slowly. The ten minute death makes you remember all the pain you experienced or caused, Nicholi told me once. Maybe it was just another story.

Father Dimitri wanted to be alone in his grief. Elena, Tasha and Anna wanted to offer their comfort, but I insisted that they stay away. Anna felt his pain greatest, I think. Too much to be of any help to him now.

"Anna. We have to prepare for the next visitor," Tasha said. "I have a scarf that would look good on you. Better than it ever looked on me. It's important that you look good and stay warm."

Tasha's tone was respectful, even kind.

Elena, Sergei and Nicholi took care of culinary matters. The fireplace was still burning hot enough to keep a few potfuls of boiling water going. There was a plentiful supply of herbs on hand, and more than enough time to air out the aroma which gave us moral pain and secret pleasure.

I was the look-out. I wish there had been Russians to watch on the horizon. I wish I didn't have to watch Father Dimitri slash off his hair, beard, and two fingers. It was something he had to do, maybe. I put his crucifix into my pocket, in the hope that he would ask for it back one day.

Reel 11

"Mozart?" I asked the Major sometime in the early afternoon. I was playing miserably that morning, my bow striking out notes, not music. Had I been playing for money on the streets, I would have owed a year's wages to the people who passed by.

I knew the Major was in the mood for something with more depth to it than Mozart. Something closer to the inner fire of life. Brahms, Beethoven, Chopin, Schubert. Even Strauss.

But I needed to play Mozart. "You have to be a virgin to play Mozart," my mother told me many times. Music flowed out of her fingers, even when she played with spoons and pots in the kitchen. She always made the best music when she was happy. I always made the best when I was enraged. Or depressed. Maybe if you play happy notes hard enough, you'll stop being depressed, I thought, as I stood in that room with the man who could save or destroy everyone and everything I ever valued.

The Major was understanding. He nodded, then started to play. The chords were the last thing I needed to hear. 'Mozart's Requiem', his most solemn and intense composition.

But such were the rules of the game. One of us chose the composer, the other the tune. Variations of tone and melody we did as we went along, of course. We must have written a hundred new sonatas and symphonies when we improvised, but I could never remember them well enough to write them down. Only two of us heard them. A special fact to the Major, a tragic one to me.

The Major sang along, his voice haunting, mesmerizing. A peacefulness so strong that it made you welcome death as the door to a life, far beyond anything we could imagine as Paradise.

I prepared myself, then took up my bow, backing up his chords and voice with harmonies above and below the melody. I was overcome with serenity. I was ready for whatever would happen next. Except for one thing. Laughter, loud and enthusiastic, echoed against the silence.

Why was the Major laughing, doubled over with unbridled joy? Was he that insightful? That sadistic?

I couldn't understand the joke the Major was laughing at. Maybe it was a joke you had to feel, not understand. But the Major understood me, I think.

He caressed the keys of the piano. Out of it came "Twinkle, Twinkle, Little Star," as most of the world knows it now. Pure Mozart. Simple, direct. A piece that forced Springtime on a tired soul.

We must have played for hours, not stopping for insignificant things like defecating, urinating, or returning warped E strings which were now C strings, and vice versa. We played to the mice in the field, the birds in the sky, and the angels above. All were listening, I think. Then, it came. The knock at the door.

Denesovic was there, on schedule. The usual time. And with the usual compensation, two hard biscuits, a piece of fruit, and the core of cabbage left from the soup of the day. All surrounding two slivers of meat, barely enough to chew, but enough to remind me of why Denesovic was still keeping us alive.

Telenkov was working out well for Denesovic, all things considered. As long as we could provide him with enough variety of chicken every night, and he could provide enough chicken steaks to the black market to ensure a Party position somewhere "civilized." We had, indeed, earned ourselves a place in the new Soviet Republic.

All of it, of course, depended on keeping the Major alive, in whatever world he was living in. We asked few questions of each other. It was like that, then. Those who asked fewer questions stayed alive longer.

The world around us was crumbling. The convoys loaded with dead "pox" victims were full, the disease too contagious for us to see how many were in the horse-drawn carts and trucks. Occasionally, prisoners would be trucked in. They were walking skeletons who would die before they reached their destination, if God was still answering their prayers. It was hardest to watch the trucks that carried one or two prisoners than those filled to capacity, in some strange way. But our responsibility was for our village, our friends, our children. In the days when our daily miseries were small enough to understand and enjoy, I wondered if the suffering of one was supposed to make you grieve as much as the suffering of many.

It was different for all of us. Sergei got numb to it all. "I'm in charge of the madness," he would say. "At least a little bit of it."

It was his job to do the butchering. Meat was meat. "Just like pigs, hens or squirrels," he claimed so many times as he skinned, gutted, and packaged dead Bolsheviks in less time than it took the best hunters in Telenkov to take the hide off a deer.

Sergei could have used a saw, but preferred his knife. "I can see what I'm doing. Feel how the meat cuts under the blade. A knife blade tells you where to cut if you listen to it," he said, with the kind of smile that has a special kind of tragedy behind it.

"People who don't value anything are less than people. They are worse than dead." Elena remembered Nadia's words, all too well. There was not much left that Sergei valued, but he did value the horses, somewhere inside him.

Maybe it was the memory of a happy, distant childhood with his uncle Ivan. Maybe it was the dream of saving his country in a final charge against evil, mounted atop a 30-year-old sway-backed gelding who still thought of himself as an undefeated 5-year-old stallion.

"The horses," Elena said to Sergei one morning, as he blankly stared out the window again. "I think I saw them. We can go there. I'll get my coat. And your old bridle."

Sergei looked out the window, self-absorbed, seeking a solution that would work for all of us. Though the biggest braggart in Telenkov, he was not one to talk much about his real problems, even in the best of times.

"I'll be back in a moment," Elena said.

By the time she returned, Sergei finally saw a solution to his problem, and ours. His knife lay in his belly.

Next to his bloody hand, a note. "Take my body. It can feed the children."

Sergei had taken care of everything. A note in his own handwriting confessed to killing the fifteen Soviet soldiers who had gone AWOL. His accounts of how he killed them were so detailed that even Nicholi would have believed them. He even managed to steal some money from the Soviets. Three years of an officer's black market wage. Enough to take care of Elena and his three daughters, wherever they were.

Sergei had anticipated everything, except for two things. Elena's tenacity, something she had to learn to stay married to Sergei. And Nicholi's skill as a surgeon, something he had to learn to stay alive in the labor camps, and in a hopelessly outnumbered White Army guerrilla band.

"Putting together torn guts is just like fixing a hose," Nicholi related calmly, as his hands frantically tried to put together what Sergei had botched up. "But for a butcher, you have a rotten knowledge of organ parts. You have to twist the knife after it goes in. And you missed the intestine."

It was a miracle that the blade missed the intestines, one that Nicholi was grateful for. He stayed with Sergei for as long as it took for each 'dissection'. I think Nicholi enjoyed using his skills to help people again, instead of to kill them. Had he not become a rotten carpenter, he would have become a great doctor.

Sergei recovered quickly, but he would try again. He had set in motion too many things for him to continue living. If the Soviets didn't come for him, they would come for one of us.

"I want to die an honorable death. One that means something," he related to me sometime after midnight. It was a moonless night, very calm and still. The kind of night where wishes are granted to those who want them hard enough.

I heard the whinny of a horse outside. "Azure?" Sergei said. He was surprised that he recognized the ghost's voice. He was astounded that the spirit was real.

Elena had led the horse all the way back from the secret hiding place she found for the herd. Where it was, I didn't ask. She wouldn't have told me, anyway.

She had risked bullets, frostbite, and the life of Azure for one reason - Sergei.

"Take him. As far from this place as you have to," Elena said.

Sergei's eyes lit up. Life spirit penetrated into every part of his body, except the part that related to women.

Sergei had not taken his second rite of passage, the journey away from the home he built for his family. Not everyone was destined to take such quests, but Sergei was one of them. Elena didn't know it when she married him, and, to be fair, Sergei didn't know it either.

Sergei stood six feet four when standing on the ground, barely eight feet when sitting in the saddle. But he was a changed man. The right one to send out, and the right time to send him.

Maybe if somebody in the outside world knew what was going on, it would stop. Another "maybe," but maybes were all we had. The Russians had guns, we had Spirits. And the spirit of the horse was the most powerful, at least for Sergei.

"He'll be back," Elena told me, as Sergei rode off into the black horizon. She smiled, absorbing her pain, hoping that it would transform her hopes into reality.

Reel 12

"When bad things happen, that's when God loves you. When good things happen, you are being set up by the devil." It was an old saying. One that Nadia the gypsy said from experience. One that Father Dimitri had told us whenever we were getting out of his control.

March started with lots of good things. Elena was in charge of the chicken distribution. She told Captain Denesovic that Sergei had left Telenkov to find a better cook. One that was even better at roasting chicken, and one that promised to reveal to Denesovic the culinary secrets of the Ancients. Anna gave Elena the names of some Indian gods and goddesses to embellish the story, with tales about Hindu hell and heaven.

Denesovic waited for the Master cook to emerge from the woods when the time was right, as Elena promised. In the meantime, we kept delivering more meat.

Our quota for chicken increased by more than ten times each week, it seemed. But it seemed that each week, ten times more Soviet soldiers came to the Miller's Cottage, all deserving to die a hundred times more. Another one of life's coincidences, I thought.

We were allowed to survive. We also became Denesovic's partners in a black market meat distribution program, which Johan calculated out to be a very profitable enterprise. If the winter were to last till May, Denesovic could buy himself any village he wanted. If the ground stayed hard till July, he could buy his way out of Ukraine and Russia.

We were even paid with money. True, inflation had made rubles worthless, even in Moscow. But getting a steady wage made us feel legitimate. As valid as anyone else in the USSR, making a profit off of someone else's misfortune.

It felt good. We were going to burn in hell, anyway, just like other "non-Chosen" people on the Earth. We didn't feel "special" anymore. We weren't suffering in that special way we used to.

Barely one in ten Soviets left the Miller's Cottage inside his boots. The rest became sausages, flanks, wieners, and soup.

The soup was particularly good. You just had to remember not to look at the eyes or the skinned head when cooking it.

"Marbles. Maybe we could use the eyes as marbles. A new toy. They would sell better than ice in July," Johan said to me on a late-night trial shift, in which another nameless Soviet soldier was found guilty. If anyone could turn a ghoulish idea into a profitable business venture, it was Johan. He was becoming a very good capitalist, but only if someone else did the selling for him.

"No, use the eyes as earrings," Tasha suggested. "To scare off the Spirits...or men with no conviction." Tasha's sexual inclinations were becoming more obvious, her tongue licking her lips as she watched Anna undress a new client-entree.

Father Dimitri did come back to help us condemn the guilty and free the innocent. But he was quiet.

There's nothing more tragic than a man who ceases to believe in himself or the cause he has dedicated his life to, and Dimitri was as dead as a man could get. Several times, Nicholi would try to goad Dimitri into an argument about politics, philosophy, or God. "You're right, Nicholi," were the only words I heard Dimitri say for weeks.

Father Dimitri tore up his priestly garb, converting them into rags. All icons and crucifixes were melted down or sold. I even caught him trying to burn his Bible, something he could not quite do yet but would get around to soon enough.

Dimitri's vote on a soldier's innocence or guilt was something he took very seriously, and he used fact, instead of theological rhetoric, to make up his mind.

It took him a long time to make up his mind, too. Once he did, he stuck firm to his vote. On more than one occasion, the rest of us voted a man guilty only to have

Dimitri put his thumb up. His explanations were brief, often unintelligible, but they were connected to a compassionate kind of logic he was teaching himself. Forgiveness and free thinking were new to ex-Father Dimitri, I think. It took some getting used to.

Elena, as usual, kept the pain and confusion to herself. "Sergei would be back," she kept telling herself again and again in the hope that it would come true. Nadia told Elena that if she could visualize Sergei riding home in her head hard enough, the Spirits would make it happen. It was something women did a lot in those times.

I found myself watching it all happen. Even though I was in the center of it all, and would ultimately direct where it was all going.

Reel 12 Continued

I always liked mornings. There was a magic few minutes when you had a sense of what you should be doing and why. Between the time of waking up and having the world's troubles thrust upon you. Anna said it had something to do with the lungs getting "Heavenly Chi." I just liked mornings.

It was March 6th. Denesovic's detail knocked on my door, to escort me to the Major for the day's music.

Denesovic's uniform was freshly pressed, his boots polished. There was an ascot around his neck, bright blue, loosely tied in the manner of a wild Cossack horseman or Siberian bandit. By the look in his eyes, I knew that the noose was waiting for Denesovic's neck, the hanging time noted somewhere in a book in the Kremlin. It was just a matter of time, now. But Denesovic wouldn't give the executioner the satisfaction of begging.

When life has no meaning, you put value on the moment of death. Denesovic would be proud, defiant. The way we all hoped ours would be.

"Chicken Telenkovian. A family recipe. It should stay in the family. We should be careful about its ingredients," Denesovic said to me out of the corner of his mouth.

With that, Denesovic left me at the door to the Major's headquarters. A car pulled up, the kind that usually didn't stop in our village. Denesovic entered, quiet and dignified.

Maybe Denesovic knew all along. Maybe he found out too late. Maybe he loved money more than Johan, and hated the Bolshevik Army as much as we all did.

It was like my best friend got taken away. A friend I just met. It was like that then, strangers and enemies becoming the best of friends just before the moment of death.

The soldiers escorted me up toward the Major's study. They were silent, terrified of the cobwebs. Each day, a detail was sent in to clean out the house top to bottom. Each night, the spiders would rebuild the webs. A natural event that we had taken for granted, like all the other miracles around us.

"The Spirits protect the spiders!" Anna told one of the few Russians we spared. The more evil the soldier, the more he feared the Spirits. My escorts ducked their heads as they passed the webs lining the roof of the squeaking staircase. I saw one of them cross himself. It was strange to see Russians grabbing hold of a belief in God after we had forfeited ours.

Denesovic had learned that things went better for everyone if the Major was happy. What made the Major happiest was music.

Denesovic had arranged for a viola, cello, harpsichord, flute, and even an old harp to be delivered to the study. They gave the old man great joy. His music became more beautiful every day. But on that day, there was only anger in the music. A rage that could not be quenched. A frustration that only he could work out, in his own way, and in his own time.

I listened to the Major play for an hour, maybe longer. I joined in, but as soon as I did, he would change the tempo, then the tune. So, I listened. And looked.

On his desk, a letter from an informer, simply signed "Igor." A detailed account. There were lots of numbers in it. The number of soldiers who had deserted. The number of officers and recruits who had visited Anna. And the number of rubles in Denesovic's very secret bank account.

The Major felt betrayed, the worst kind of pain for a man with his pride and honor. How could a junior officer whom he treated like a son make a mockery of his command? True, the Major and Denesovic protected each other in a world gone mad, but in the Major's world, an honest answer was the only true one. The only one you get from a real friend.

But what would the Major think of the US? What would he do to us? And to himself, when he figured it all out?

It was a dangerous time for asking real questions and giving honest answers. But the Major gave us no choice. The day of reckoning was at hand.

CHAPTER 9

Geoff was too tired to be exhausted, a feeling he hadn't had for a long time. It felt good to be dedicated to something again, even though he didn't know what it was.

An envelope came through the delivery chute. A Fax, "Doctor Weinburg. You are to cooperate with the Russian authorities. It's a matter of international security." The stationery was from the National Institutes of Health, Communicable Disease Branch. The signature: "George."

It could have been George Richardson, Harvard colleague and head of the Institute, who never refused Geoff a single grant request in 15 years, despite a kill ratio of 40:1 for anyone else. A closer look at the swirls on the signature revealed something more ominous.

George and Barbara had invited Geoff to the house for supper on two occasions. It was tacky to accept an autographed photo of you with the President, but it was necessary for the grant prospectus. Maybe the signature on the Fax was a forgery, Geoff thought. The Russian Mafia and KGB had teamed up on more than one project in the past. But two things were certain. Bush had been director of the CIA before his Vice-Presidential and Presidential career, and he was not the kind of person who took 'no' for an answer. And not even superstars like Geoff could go up against the KGB, the Mob, or the CIA without incurring some major league damage.

"You can walk out of here, Geoff," Yakov related. "Still time for YOU to come out of this with your ass and sanity intact. Who'll be around to pervert another generation of scientists if BOTH of us wind up in a psychiatric facility for a diagnostic 20-year check-up?"

"What about the force field around this place? They can't come in. We can't go out, Yakov."

"Taken care of. The Southwest fence between the kitchen and the motor pool. A hole they haven't discovered yet."

"A trap door, Yakov? You Soviets are undignified and unpoetic. Did the defenders of the Alamo have a back door to make a getaway from Santa Ana's army?"

"They did, Geoff."

"And did anyone take it?"

"One man. A Frenchman. He lived a long life. A happy one too, all things considered."

"Right. The coward. The one that didn't stand and fight. Like Jim Bowie. Davy Crockett."

"Mister Crockett got shot in the back. Trying to run away after the Mexicans stormed the walls. So did at least fifty others."

"You've been reading too many Soviet history books, Yakov. The Alamo was about saying 'fuck off' to authority!!!"

"It was about gold, Geoff. A whole pile of gold the defenders were going to save for themselves."

"Stop fucking around, Yakov!!! You have a point to all of this?!!!"

"I don't know!!!"

Yakov was too worried to continue arguing. Geoff wavered between fear and bravado, hoping to find courage and perhaps clear thinking somewhere in the middle.

"I'll keep talking, only if the American wants to listen," Boris said to Yakov.

Boris continued. "The first skirmish tests your defiance. The willingness to charge the demon's defenses a second time tests your courage. You have to know that the devil's bullets hurt before you know if you are afraid of them."

The words and subtexts were translated for Geoff. True to the old Ukrainian's words, Geoff turned catatonic.

Suddenly, another round of bullets was fired. Windows broke, plaster pounded down. Geoff ducked for cover, Yakov and Boris laughing like it was a shower of leaves on a windy autumn afternoon.

"One battery down. But they won't kill us. Not until the last two batteries protecting this place run out," Yakov commanded.

"Which will be...?"

"Three, maybe five more tapes. All that we need, I think."

"Hmmm", Geoff said to himself, contemplative. He nodded his head. "Salt in my mouth. Why do I taste salt in my mouth?"

"Because you've already wet your pants. And it's judgment day. The air tastes salty every judgment day." Boris said.

"I've had enough of these Goddamn riddles, you fuckin'...fuckin'!!!" Geoff didn't know what to call the old man whom he finally had the courage to grab by the collar.

Boris smiled, then splattered out something in Ukrainian.

"Anger is good. A better alternative to fear. A wrong decision is better than no decision." Yakov translated. "What's your decision?" he added.

Geoff scribbled something on an envelope and shoved it into the outbound chute to Hartunian before Yakov could peek at it, and before Boris could intuit what message he had sent to the outside world.

"I want to keep YOU two guessing for a little while," Geoff said. He sat down, tried to straighten the wrinkles in his trousers, crossed his legs, and looked at his watch. "Ten minutes. On a sabbatical to India, I gave God five minutes to tell me why I should listen to him. I'll give you two assholes ten to tell me why I should listen to you."

The shoe was on the other foot. Yakov had big feet. Boris had flexible toes. Both were nervous and started to second-guess the validity of bringing the most arrogant scientist West of the Atlantic into the best-kept secret East of the Baltic.

Reel 12

We froze, terrified to open the door of our communal "feast hall" the day after my last visit to the Major's study. But the visitor kept knocking, several times.

We took a silent vote in the spirit of our newly found democracy. Elena was elected to answer the door. She approached slowly.

"The Major walks softly, and knocks loudly," Nicholi noted.

"God will do to us what He has to," Father Dimitri commented.

"I suppose we'll all get what's coming to us today," Nicholi said. "We'll all get what we deserve today, Father."

Nicholi threw Dimitri a crucifix, one he had carved out of the pine wood. Pinewood was rare, but it symbolized long life.
The depiction of Jesus on the cross had bad body proportions, but kind eyes.

Dimitri put the crucifix around his neck, out of gratitude to Nicholi. He crossed himself, thankful to God, in the event that He still existed.

Suddenly, there was a loud knock, one that sounded like finality. Elena answered the door. Behind it, the wind, howling through the barren landscape from the North. And a woodpecker, eating a hole in the rotted wood.

"Well, is that what's become of the Major?" Johan said.
If that's the case, our troubles are over."

Johan needed to tell a joke. We needed to laugh. Everyone except me.

"He'll be here. The Major told me he would be here at two o'clock. According to the invitation we gave him," I said, gazing at my pocketwatch, a gift secretly given to me by Denesovic so I would not miss any of the sessions with the Major. Denesovic said it was confiscated from a band of Kurdish Moslems, a mystical sect who tried to wage a Holy War against the Red Army. He said that it would run on time, every day. Until the day that my time ran out.

I watched the seconds tick away, hoping that my eyes could see what my heart was feeling. Time didn't stop for us, but it slowed down. The Spirits were not kind enough to be too obvious with us.

True to his word, the Major appeared in the doorway. Under his left arm was a violin, in his right hand, a basket.

"Boris?" he said, "I brought some dried fruit and nuts. A little something for luck."

To come to a feast empty-handed in the Major's world was bad form, and bad form was unacceptable anywhere. Invited guests had obligations, too.

We feared the Major. The children liked him. There was a secret between them that was not shared with us.

I didn't tell you about the children, I know. We kept them close to us, but as far away from what was happening as we could. I would rather not speak of them. It is too painful for me to remember. You will know why - soon enough.

"A song, play us a song," the children asked the Major. He was all too obliging. He played every request, the strings on the violin penetrating into souls, his voice finding a special place in our hearts.

Nicholi admired the music's boldness, the ability to inspire you to be better than what you are. Johan shed a tear; the Major's repertoire included some Polish tunes from his Native land, a place he knew he would never see again. Elena was moved by the love songs, in special ways that could only be enjoyed by women. With Anna and Tasha, it was about friendship. How much they shared as lovers, or wanted to, was their own business. But it was as special as any other relationship. Father Dimitri never really liked music, but he could be moved by it easily. I think that music restored his faith in God.

We had prepared some "legitimate" food, rations allowed to us by the Russians, officially. We had become experts in making the portions look larger than they really were. Then there was an added entree, which was much more controversial.

If overcooked and smothered with enough "secret ingredients," you could hide the taste of anything, even human meat. Garlic, sage and basil worked best. We also discovered new, exotic ways to make the flesh of our fellow human beings taste "legitimate." Intestines, brains, bone meal, extracts from the eyes, and lungs had an odor of their own, distinctive enough to be sold as anything to an unsuspecting guest.

While Father Dimitri had been paying for his earthy sins in a worldly purgatory, Nicholi had taken over as our leader in spiritual matters. He suggested that we serve Chicken Telenkovian to the Major. "We have to see what he does. How he reacts to it. With his heart, his eyes, and his mind."

Nicholi was never as eloquent as Father Dimitri, but he was right. None of us knew the Major, even me. Maybe he didn't even know himself. Madness is like that, Nadia told me many times.

Anna served the entree, cut into slices. "A big bird. A loner hawk, I think. Maybe an owl," she said. "He got lost here and was too hurt to return home."

The Major appreciated the truth, even if it was cloaked in a well-intended lie. Corporal Korsikoff was a loner, dedicated to serving a cause - himself. He was cruel, but not vicious. Maybe we saved the world from another Stalin by killing this twenty-year-old model recruit, who kept the front teeth of his victims on a chain around his neck. Or maybe Korsikoff would have outgrown his boyhood fad of cruelty and become the man who would save the Soviet Union from inevitable disaster.

If only we could have served "Igor" to the Major. We would have found out who the informer was within a few days. Anna could determine his next move in a matter of minutes.

As the invited guest, the Major took the first bite of Telenkovian fowl, according to his custom and ours.

With the first bite, he nodded in approval. With the second, he complimented the chef. With the third, a hard swallow.

"Korsikoff," he said, recognizing the source of the meat. He was somber, reflective, and compassionate. He pointed to the other entrees, naming them according to the 'bad apple' soldier they had come from. He then got up. "Everyone, eat. Please. I prefer to play."

I recognized the tune he played on my violin. Beethoven's Opus 135. A work so beautiful, it made the highest Angel appreciate the struggles of the lowest man. Heaven and earth were brought closer together with each note. Each of us could see the face of God more clearly with each measure. It was a different face for each of us, in accordance with what we valued most in ourselves and each other.

I could hear the silence, too. The silence between the notes. It's something that only happens when the listener and player work together.

The last movement on paper was only ten minutes long, but the Major stretched it out to at least an hour. Improvised endings could be changed into beginnings. No one got tired of it. There were still more layers to add.

I closed my eyes and offered my soul to God. If He, or It, were to take me now, that would be all right. The blackness in front of my eyes was giving way to a bright light, a door that lay open in front of me many times. "Take me, now," I felt my soul screaming in ecstasy. "Into Your hands, I commend my spirit. Thy Will be done!!!"

My prayers were answered, in a way I never expected.

The music stopped. I opened my eyes. In front of me, the Major, collapsed. With his last ounce of physical strength, he put the violin in my trembling hands.

"Please. Finish it," he said to me.

I never saw a man more in control of his own death. Whether it was the Spirits who saw fit to end the Major's stay with us, or whether it was a cyanide capsule, I will never know.

"Play me up to the stars," the Major repeated. He was happy, I think. Maybe the first time in his life when he was happy and aware of his surroundings, both at the same time.

It was the greatest honor bestowed upon me, the most painful thing I ever did. And the most joyous. "Pain and pleasure are the same thing," I remember from somewhere. I had never experienced both more intensely. I started from the beginning.

By the time I reached the last passage, the Major smiled. I tried to make the last note last as long as it could, but it had to end. So did the Major's stay in the land of the living. But not before he said something in Greek. The only Greek I knew which Father Dimitri said when giving us communion. "Eat of my body, drink of my blood."

The Major fell to the ground quickly. His face turned white before our eyes, as if his ghost knew it had to leave quickly. It's supposed to take three days for the soul to leave the body, according to our traditions. But the Major's soul knew something we didn't.

All of us were moved. Tears were in everyone's eyes, save Nicholi's. "The dead deserve to be let go so that they can move on," he said. Nicholi hurt more inside than anyone else, I think. He couldn't shed a single tear. If he ever let the floodgates open, it would never stop. It was the only way he could handle the death of someone he cared about.

I looked at my pocket watch. It had stopped. Maybe it was because the Major fell on it, the logical explanation.

From outside, we heard trucks. A few were leaving, a lot more coming in. It was time to get out and to cover our tracks.

"The Major deserves an appropriate burial," I said, "By people who care about him."

What we did next we did out of love We would regret it for the rest of our lives. You will too.

CHAPTER 10

Finality. It was the only word that echoed through Geoff's mind, the only thought that penetrated into his soul.

The external data well justified the internal hypothesis. The phone wires into and out of the complex were cut down. Military vehicles and ambulances encircled the compound, blocking any view of the woods. From above, choppers hovered, like vultures, waiting for a hole in the defense field.

Yakov did well to improve on the security, which had been designed around this biological research station, which had been used for many purposes over the years, sometimes as a mental hospital, sometimes as a place to store nuclear warheads or chemical weapons, now too expensive to destroy. Sometimes it was used to store wheat, a valued commodity in a country where food was scarce and tensions were high.

Yakov's biomagnetic force field around the complex was Nobel Prize-winning stuff. A twenty-fifth century transformation of matter to anti-matter, that could be maintained as long as nineteenth century batteries could put out enough electrical juice. It was Yakov's best work. His final Opus, composed for a special occasion in which Geoff would be the star performer, whether he wanted to be or not.

And Geoff was being transformed by the music around him into a man he never was, or never imagined could exist in the real world. He was here for a purpose, he thought, but what? Geoff was always an in-control kind of guy. In the last eight hours, he had experienced emotions he had denied or pushed away for a lifetime. Fear, horror, and love.

"Someone has a very hidden agenda here," Geoff protested. "Boris. What's your hidden agenda?"

The old man gathered the reserves of his composure and smoked a cigarette. The last one in the pack, which he would smoke at his own pace, on his own terms.

Frustrated, beyond his limit, Geoff turned to Yakov.

"Yakov. Damn it! What's going on here? We're supposed to be rational. Thinking with our heads, not our feelings. The kind of people who solve problems. Not controlled by situations." Still, more frustrating silence. "You're holding out on me. You're gonna get all of us

killed, Yakov. We're supposed to be friends. You're the only friend I've got left!!!"

Geoff concluded Yakov that he had been putting aside for half a lifetime. It was hard to face the fact that the closest friend Geoff ever had was half a world away. Maybe that was why Yakov had remained a friend. Maybe that was why Yakov could remain a friend. He knew how to avoid Geoff's self-sabotage of any friendship that came his way.

Yakov was true to his nature and Geoff's expectations.

"Friends don't give other friends ultimatums, Geoff. You're right."

Yakov scribbled out a note. A diagram outlining the escape route. "An underground tunnel out of here. Twice the length of the Lincoln Tunnel and, I am afraid, a hundred times smellier. But there is a car at the other side. With enough gas in the tank to get you out of the State. Enough papers to get you out of the country. And a numbered account in a Swiss bank. A travel fund that the Ministry of Science has been keeping. Better that YOU get it, than the SOVIET capitalists. Or the mobsters."

Geoff pondered. One more look over the edge.

"It's not your fight, Geoff. I realize that now. It's mine. And his." Yakov pointed to Boris.

Boris' eyes were calm. It was Geoff's decision now. The line drawn in the sand in the Alamo before the Mexicans attacked was made to give men options, not to intimidate them into false bravado, Geoff thought. Besides, the world was falling apart anyway. The entire "System" was designed, consciously or unconsciously, to maintain a high standard of living for the top 3%. One person couldn't change the system, Geoff thought. The best you could do was to get yourself, or your friends, into the 3% that ruled everybody else. Geoff was already on top and, once Yakov had completed his suicide mission-whatever it was -, he would have no friends to share the throne with. For Geoff, there was now nothing to gain and everything to lose. No matter what he did.

Geoff hesitated. Another variable, he hoped - and prayed - for. Another "something" that would let reason dictate what he should do, and provide an answer to it all.

The clock ticked down on Yakov's make-shift power supply for the force field. Matching Japanese, German, American, and Russian parts was the big trick, and there wasn't enough time to build it according to the ideal design. Nine hours and twelve tapes' worth of power was all that Yakov could come up with. Maybe that was the idea. An idea planted by Boris.

After another look at Boris, a visceral realization infiltrated through all of Geoff's protective walls. Suddenly, Geoff could FEEL the fading vision in his fiery eyes. Geoff could VIBRATE to the tremors the old man struggled to fight every time he lifted up a cigarette to his mouth. SMELL the smoke coming out of his face, one that was deformed on one side because of damage to the colossal fibers between the cerebral hemispheres. He could SEE the air coming into and out of 90-year-old lungs, kept open by muscles which were in advanced stages of degeneration. TOUCH the pressure receptors on his skin, which wanted to feel the world, but couldn't. The nerves going to them had been destroyed by an endogenous toxin, produced by a neurological disease that had no name in the textbooks, but which seemed very familiar.

Geoff felt alive. Like a healer, not just a doctor. Then, a flash.

"Animal models of disease," Geoff said. "What animal models of this disease have we seen?" Geoff crumpled up the paper, revealing the way to his escape route.

Yakov smiled. Geoff was entitled to know the whole story now. He hugged Geoff the way Russians hug comrades. Americans never hug, Geoff thought. Not unless they want to pick your pocket, one way or another.

Yakov went to a safe, hidden in the corner. "One, two, three," Yakov muttered, as he twisted the combination on a lock tied to a hidden plastic explosive. "A simple combination. I can only remember simple things these days."

Yakov presented Geoff with a box. "Happy birthday, my friend." The wrapping was a collage of pages from Pravda, the New York Times, The National Enquirer, and a centerfold that would be considered erotic art in Budapest, but triple-X smut in any American courtroom. Boris sang "Happy Birthday" to Geoff, joined in by Yakov. Both sang with voices made drunk by desperation and courage.

Geoff was not impressed. "Stop fucking around with my head!!! Stop fucking around with my head...." he screamed in futility. Then, in the middle of the third verse, he ripped open the package. In it - more paper. Some pages parched, some new, some faded so much that print and page melded together, hiding secrets only knowable to someone who would read them with determined eyes. Then, another box inside.

Geoff tore it open. Much to read, he thought. Boris started to talk again. Much more to listen to, Geoff realized. Better to listen than read, Geoff intuited. If he was going to die, the "whys" were more important than the "hows."

CHAPTER 11

The recorder jammed. There was no movement of the German-made wheels, inside the Japanese-manufactured frame, that had been put together in a Leningrad factory. Just a buzz, drilling a hole into Yakov's brain to the core of his rage and unending frustration. A sadistic reward for trying to do the right thing, in a world that seemed to be designed to go more wrong with each passing year.

Boris smiled soberly. "Divine retribution and justice," he related. "Some things are supposed to be known in the heart, not on the record."

"It wasn't supposed to happen like this. When I brought you over here, WE were supposed to be in control. WE were going to save the world from itself," Yakov related between screams and curses. But ten years of schooling in bioelectronics was no match for the self-sabotage that seemed to be built into any piece of Soviet machinery.

"Scrapies. Mad Cow disease. You and your kids got scrapies from eating the Major," Geoff said. The symptoms fit the history on his chart. Delayed incubation period. Ataxia, fluctuating sensory dysfunction. Short-term memory deficits. Schizophrenic psychosis with hallucinations and lesions in the temporal lobes.

"You're a very smart man," Boris said to Geoff. "I hope you are a courageous one, too." It was a meeting of the minds and the souls.

"How many OTHER people got scrapies from eating the Major's brain?" Geoff asked.

"Everyone...I think," Boris related. "We all ran away. Some got out, some didn't. We tried to write letters to each other, but..."

The old man turned quiet again. The military vehicles outside became noisier. The clock ticked down on the two force-field batteries that kept anything made of flesh or steel out of the compound. The messages had piled up in the mail chute. Some had the humor of a Far Side comic, designed to appeal to Geoff's reason. Some had offers he couldn't refuse, aimed at his greed. Some were overtly stern, reminding him that he who designs the guns makes the law, but he who holds the trigger on the guns rules people. "Surrender the prisoner or suffer with him," was the subtext of them all.

"Two minutes left," Yakov said with a calm voice and trembling heart, as the clock on the power source ticked down. "Then all we can do is bluff. I'm good at getting and deciphering unofficial information. We were trained to have top-level analytical minds. But bluffing is something you learn on the streets. Neither of us spent any time on the streets, Geoff. Those people out there did."

Geoff was well aware of what Yakov meant, and the irony here. All scientists lived in constant fear of being "found out." That day the world would find out that you got to where you were at because you were lucky in trying to outguess nature, or outmanoeuver scientific colleagues for research dollars or professional status points. The villagers outside the castle walls knew something far more powerful than advanced calculus or quantum mechanics. They knew how to face real life.

Could Geoff really deal with life in a political prison, a mental institution, or remain sane in that corridor between life and death at the hands of an executioner? That executioner could be American as easily as Russian. On the payroll of KGB, CIA, the Mafia, or General Motors.

There was one lingering question still in Geoff's head. "Why Hartunian? What's a Nobel Laureate doing out there? He's one of us."

"He WAS one of us," Yakov explained. "Doing what he had to to survive."

"By hiding and faking data since the fifties on this thing?" Geoff said.

"When Comrade Professor comes into your laboratory and asks if you have found a cure for the disease assigned to you, you say 'Yes, comrade'. 'Of course'. It's the way you keep yourself and your family alive. Do it enough, and they make you an assistant professor. More food for your family. Keep doing it again, and they will make you a full professor, then head of the institute. It is a very moral decision, as long as you spend all your time off with your OWN children and nobody else's." Yakov hesitated. "He got in 'too deep'. Starting with having worked in a laboratory creating viruses that simulated microbes that caused the Mad Cow disease epidemic in animals and people in 1924, which was, officially, stopped by Professor Doctor. Hartunian and his team. Hartunian, who was my mentor, then friend, was promoted. His career, and life of finding real cures for diseases,, has been built on too many lies, . Even if he is

officially forgiven, he could never live as a commoner. Tell me, L. Geoffrey Weinburg, M.D., Ph.D., could you be happy working in a donut shop?"

"But there's a 'why' to this!" Geoff protested. "There's got to be a 'why' to this that we can understand. It HAS to be about someone doing something to somebody else. A hidden agenda. EVERYone, even fuckin' Santa Claus, has a fucking hidden agenda!!"

From Boris, silence again. He was talked out. Yakov knew some of the details, but not the whole truth about the rest of the tragedy. It was as if he was holding on to it for someone who really had to know. Someone who had wisdom and cleverness. Both would be required to carry the torch before Boris would surrender to the disease or the Soviet authorities.

Geoff was a population-oriented kind of guy. But if Boris's wisdom taught him anything, it was that the secret of life was about being one-to-one. Yakov's courage inspired him to use that new insight.

"Anna. What happened to Anna?" Geoff asked Boris.

The old man talked. With a warm heart, a troubled spirit. "She had to continue in the profession life assigned to her, I think. The world asked her for sex, and she tried to give it love. Love still delivered through a mind gone mad, a body eaten away by disease. I think she made it as far as the Baltic. Maybe Romania. I stopped getting letters from her when the Germans invaded."

"Tasha?"

"In Telenkov, life forced us to be tolerant of women who saw more value in loving other women than men. We men do abuse women, all of us. One way or the other. The Nazis didn't see things that way. They considered her kind lower than a Jewish dog. So did the Jews. But she experienced love on her own terms before she died. Something I didn't." He remained silent, reflective again.

"Sergei...and Elena?"

"Hungary. There were lots of horses in Hungary for Sergei. Yellow flowers for Elena. A big country without any labor camps, with many possibilities. Like America.""

"Johan?"

"He ran as quickly as he could back to Poland. One day he ran too fast, and got shot in the back. He was lucky. His soul was too weak to live with madness, and too undeveloped to appreciate it."

"Nicholi."

"He became a surgeon. A healer. While his hands still worked, he saved many people. Then he became a

mental patient in his own hospital. But, I hear, his patients took good care of him."

"Father Dimitri."

"Tibet. India. The monasteries in the high mountains in Turkey. Some say he went there. I don't know. Maybe he chose a harder spiritual path - taking a wife and raising a family."

"And the rest?" Geoff asked.

A pause.

"The rest, I do not know too much about. Labor camps. Bullets. Cold exposure. Starvation. Suicide. Disease. There are many ways to die here. All ugly. The Major's madness made so many see beautiful things before dying. Sometimes. But, life gives us joy in brief 'sometimes'. Somehow, it's the way it works. Life always balances itself."

Boris smiled. Another "sometime" moment. The end was coming for him, one way or the other. He looked forward to the visions the Major saw in front of his eyes before dying. But still, it was dying.

"It's a NEW strain of scrapies," Yakov commented. "Far more vicious above the neck than between the ears. It can turn you into an Einstein. Then a blabbering idiot.

Then a rabid dog, who lives in three time zones and five worlds, most of them of your own creation."

"Like a chairman of a biophysics department, or a network executive," Geoff added. He chuckled a bit. Yakov's approval could have turned it into a much-needed laugh. Something to give him a moment of control so that he could deal with the panic around and inside him. Yakov did not accommodate his old friend's desperate request.

"War leaves behind very contagious memories," Yakov related. "The influenza virus after World War I. Soldiers brought back home a lot more than bad memories. Millions died from the flu epidemic in 1919. Only a fraction of that number died in the Great War. Every soldier who survived the battlefield brought home a heart full of horrible memories, and a lung full of deadly viruses."

"So how contagious WAS this mad cow and mad human thing?"

"You mean how contagious IS it?"

Shock in Geoff's eyes. Yakov continued.

"It was under control in the fifties. Like AIDS in your military is now."

Shock turned to horror. Geoff was well aware that in the mid-eighties, fifteen percent of the West Point cadets were HIV positive, a tip from Susan Hasselback, a lab tech who came in and out of Geoff's life on HIS timetable. Susan never lied about data or her feelings. Geoff was more concerned with his career at the time than yet another venereal disease that would cull the population of military grunts.

"I can believe that Soviet KGB yahoos invented country music to kill American brain cells," Geoff said, still able to hide behind the cleverness of language, "But I can't believe that the worldwide problem today is all because of a virus that eats gray matter in the cranial vault."

"But you do believe in statistics," Yakov retorted. His claim was backed up with reams of data he pulled out of the safe and dumped on the table. Hundreds of cases of this new brand of scrapies in people and animals.. Russian. Baltic. German. South African. And clusters smuggled out of Western Canada and Iowa. All well documented. All dead.

"What do they want with Boris?" Geoff asked.

"His brain. The Major spent a summer on a sheep farm near a veterinary laboratory, just after the Revolution. His job was to protect the sheep from wild dogs. The sheep all died. Maybe he got the virus from the sheep. Maybe someone made it in the laboratory. Maybe military people

were experimenting with virus warfare long before we scientists knew about viruses. The virus is an embarrassment. A political disease."

"And an economic one?" Geoff asked. "Russia wants to export sheep on the international market at top prices." Yakov's silence revealed the unspoken truth. Geoff didn't have to remind Yakov that a few cases of scrapies in Scottish sheep nearly bankrupted the British meat industry. And that the only reason why Canadian beef was supporting the wheat belt was because the veterinary community was smart enough to keep reports of Brucillosis infection in cattle away from anything in print.

"Damn it, Yakov. The Canadians were smart-or clever-enough to kill off most of the bison still left in Western Canada because someone THOUGHT that Brucellosis infection was in a few buffalo, and COULD affect beef prices." Geoff was indignant, angry. For perhaps the first time in his life, he was angry at someone who deserved it, for a cause other than himself. "The Canadians KILLED the biggest herd of bison in the fuckin' world in the Wood Buffalo Park's test and cull program. At least the Canadians stopped at killing BUFFALO. Are you assholes over here so pathetic that you'd hide a deadly

human disease, so you can get an extra nickel a pound on lamb prices on the international market?"

The communal shame and agony of the Russian people came over Yakov's face. "We've been a cursed people for a long time. You've been a lucky people, so far. We have done what we have to stay alive. You've done what you have to do to stay on top. So far."

"So...what do we do about it?"

CHAPTER 12

Boris spoke. "Before the battle between good and evil started, God let the devil have one trick. One trick he could use against a man."

"Woman?" Geoff countered.

"Lack of vision. A blindfold over the eye that lets us see the Way. A madness that makes us confuse up with down. Right with Wrong. Light with Darkness. Friend with Foe."

Boris' words were true. It pained this old man to have to say them to a younger one not yet ready to understand what they meant.

Geoff always wanted to change the world, but was not willing to be changed in the process. He was now in the driver's seat. He was now the center of power. And it's a victim.

The truth about Boris' past, and the world's future, was in Geoff's hands. Should he publicize a disease that could ruin the Soviet economy? The Soviet military fanatics always got control of the country when the civilians were hurting most, and those fanatics were capable of unleashing any kind of destruction. It was their duty, and pleasure, to punish the outside world for problems that plagued Mother Russia.

Keeping everything quiet was another option. After all, who could prove that Boris' tale of pathos and horror was real? And who would care about a few thousand people dying of a disease still out there? For that matter, who would care about the Soviet economy, once everything collapsed? The American capitalists, Mafia, and the rats would have to take their turns in sacking the once-great Soviet Empire before it would be rebuilt. Anyway, business as usual never destroyed the natural order of things in the world before, and it would not do so now, either. Then there was logic. The truth can set people free, but only brave people. Lies were always safer than the truth, at least in Geoff's world.

But logic, common sense, or even selfishness were luxuries Geoff could not afford anymore. The gods of urgency, panic, and ultimatum ruled now.

Yakov's force field around the compound was fading fast. High noon with the posse outside was barely minutes away, and they would take no prisoners - at least LIVE prisoners. The vehicles revved up their engines, and the choppers prepared for an all-out assault. Santa Anna's international army was going to storm the walls of the 20th-century Alamo any time now.

Boris wasn't holding out too well. There was a death rattle in his breathing, an unmistakable sound Geoff had heard many times during his medical internship. A sound he had desensitized himself to in the clinic. And which he had forgotten when he opened his research lab across Second Avenue in Manhattan.

What Geoff would have given for one moment of clarity. One glimpse of the world as it is, and as it should be. A single vision, unclouded by his own confusion of the conflicting opinions of others. Mystics had such visions, so he remembered reading. Maybe Boris did. And maybe Yakov was having one right now.

"Boris will make it. As far as he has to. He will live forever, no matter what happens. As for me..." Yakov's voice was calm, relaxed. He carted up the final boxes of tapes and removed a panel from the wall. Inside, a bottle of Newfoundland Screech, the 300 proof rum that sent so many Maritime sailors to sea, and drew so many safely back to port. He served it up, according to plan - almost.

"Glasses," Yakov related, as he poured the contraband Canadian brew into vintage hospital cups. "No matter how broke we Slavs are, we always can afford vodka, rum, and glasses.To your health!!!...To EVERYONE'S health."

It was the kind of toast a man drinks alone. Punctuated with a smile, a gulp, then a toss of the glass against the wall. After being emptied into Yakov's empty belly, it shattered in a million pieces. A magnificent blast! "Did you see that!!! I CAN make American plastic break like Russian crystal," Yakov smiled, proudly. He felt it to be his greatest accomplishment. And his last.

Yakov took off his shirt and trousers. There was no underwear beneath them. "The world respects a man with no hidden agenda. At least for a little while," he said to Geoff by way of explanation.

He would face the world naked now. But not unprotected.

In the closet hung a sheepskin coat, leggings, and boots.

"They were my Grandfather's. A Ukrainian chieftain whom the world called a peasant. At least that's what Boris tells me.

It makes sense. I always felt out of place in Moscow.

Even though my father said we had RUSSIAN roots back to Peter the Great." The vintage warrior gear fit loosely around Yakov's arms, tight around the waist, but right around his eyes,

From Geoff, shock. Then concern. The kind of concern reserved for the closest of brothers. The best of friends. "Yakov. Why didn't you tell me? Do you have this... disease?"

Yakov smiled. "Maybe. I think it's inherited. Maybe I WANT it to be one of those inheritable diseases. I'm getting tired of living in this dimension, anyway. Time to move on. Change careers, and perspectives."

Yakov shook Geoff's hand. Geoff was uncomfortable with hugs, even at a time like this. Geoff would have to deal with the consequences of Yakov's actions. He had a right to some distance, Yakov thought.

Geoff couldn't speak. The words were stuck in his mouth, the feeling behind them gripping his chest. "Should I cry?" he found himself stuttering.

"No. You don't have to. Not yet...," Yakov said.

Boris looked up. He opened his arms. An embrace was appropriate here. Much needed to be expressed and exchanged.

Finally, the alarm clock on the box Yakov left with Geoff ticked down to a piercing alarm sound at 'noon', or was it 'midnight'?. "No horse outside. Maybe a motorcycle will do. Take a picture. For our children. I think I may have some." Yakov speculated. After which, he gave Geoff another box. It was gift-wrapped, with black paper. Inside, a handgun. "Do with it what you have to do with it." The renegade Ukrainian scientist said. "There are people out there who want Boris' brain, with or without his soul attached to it. He's the only one who survived that Easter dinner in Telenkovian during the Holodomor. The only one who has the cure inside him. If they get him, the world as we knew it-or want to know it-will be destroyed."

It was another riddle. Was the cure Boris had in him medical, spiritual, or both? A madman could harvest enough scrapie virus from Boris' cranial vault to wipe out any country he wanted to? A humanitarian could develop an effective antibody to the deadly microbe if he were smart and connected enough. But even if Boris could be saved, what to we do with him? A lose-lose situation anyway, as Geoff saw it, from HIS perspective.

For a scientist, Yakov was as dramatic as they came. He had a knack for making even the dullest data sound interesting at scientific meetings. All, of course, was within the limits of good taste and professional protocol.

Yakov's charge into the explosives building visible from the formerly protected interrogation room on his motorcycle while clad as a mounted Cossack went well beyond good taste and protocol. The 1200 cc two-wheeled steed held the ground firm, as bullets shattered its tires and mangled its spokes. Yakov gave out a bold rebel yell, as heroic as any seen on the battlefield or simulated on any Hollywood screen.   An ecstasy of delight. It was a warrior's death, in a world where the end usually comes slow, degrading the spirit before destroying the body.

.

Then the blast. It was magnificent and horrifying to watch from where Geoff was standing.

The explosion destroyed the rows of military vehicles and tanks surrounding the compound. around the interrogation room. It was a feat of physics that would make any stunt coordinator in Moscow, Hollywood, or Delhi proud. But there was more than one row of vehicles, a calculation Yakov didn't anticipate. Behind the row of inactivated machines and mercenaries hired by the New Capitalists who would run post-Soviet Russia to kill Boris, Geoff, and all evidence of the events that happened in

Telenkovia, were two more rows of healthy men ready to carry out their bosses' orders. Such included Professor Doctor Hartunian, who miraculously survived the blast without a scratch.

A minute was all the time Geoff had to make a decision that would change the history of the world, and his innermost soul. A soul he did not know existed until now.

"God will understand, whatever you do," Boris said calmly, as machinery and men moved in from the ground and the air.

"Fuck you. Fuck God. And fuck this whole..."

Logic kicked in. Geoff found himself pointing the gun at Boris's head. "I splatter your brains across that wall, and we ALL get out of here. I go back to New York. Those assholes out there get to go back to destroying whatever third world countries are on GM and Mobil Oil's hit list. You get to go to Paradise and fuck your brains out with Anna."

"That would be nice. I'd enjoy that," Boris said. There was no coercion in his voice. Just the daydreaming of a man looking forward to a last reward. He began to sing Beethoven's Opus 135.

Geoff was paralyzed with fear. Boris stopped singing.

"Come on, Geoffrey," Boris said to his new 'handler". You have to do it. If I do, it's suicide. God doesn't allow people like me to commit suicide, I think."

He started to sing again, even louder., It was a death chant of his own making, sung joyously.

"Stop singing!!! Stop singing!!!" Geoff screamed, as footsteps echoed around him from the hallways and ground outside of the 'bunker'. Boot heels that heralded his liberators, as long as he held on to the gun, or his captors, if he let it go. Still, Boris continued to sing.

"If I shoot this thing, they'll find us in this maze!!!" Geoff screamed again. "You want them to find you dead!!!?"

The singing continued. It was the way Boris wanted it done, shot by a friend. Geoff would tell the tale. That was all Boris wanted. Someone to be left alive who knew the real story. What happened next, even Boris didn't expect.

CHAPTER 13

Boris kept his eyes closed. It would be easier that way, he thought for him and Geoff.

Five shots. Hard. Straight into the target. Geoff had shot pistols on the range, but being arm's length from a freshly-blasted bullet hole was another matter.

He stared at Boris for a second that seemed hours long. How could five pieces of metal smaller than a baby's finger destroy what it took a lifetime to build? A lifetime of careful collaborative effort between God and man, Nature and its creation.

Suddenly, the scattered drumbeats of boot heels and the clamor of doors being rammed open around the interrogation room stopped. A moment of peace. Silence. Then, urgency, at the unmistakable cadence of 2/4 double time, converged all around him.

"They did one hell of a job on Yakov's matter-antimatter generator box," Geoff said calmly. Wondrous inventions such as this would have to wait for a world that

could find better uses for them than a security system, he thought.

Boris opened his eyes. Surprised to be alive!. He hadn't been surprised in at least a decade.

"You don't die till I give you permission, you got that, old man?" Geoff swung Boris over his shoulder. This Ukrainian mentor could outstare and outsmoke anyone, but running through a tunnel of horrors ahead of crack mercenary troops was another matter.

"Papers. You have to take the papers," Boris protested. "That is what it is all about."

"You are what it's all about now."

"The papers. YOUR world needs proof. The one I'm going to..."

Boris sang again. Loud enough to be heard in Leningrad

"Okay!" Geoff said. "The papers. We'll take the fucking papers."

"And the tapes."

"And the goddamn tapes!"

Geoff loaded the papers and tapes into a backpack on which there was a Ukrainian flag, which Yakov had 'coincidently' left behind. The 40-something American scientist who had ample hair on his head but not the bubba belly most of his contemporaries developed, hoped that the training he did to look fit had made him so. His resting heart rate never went above fifty. He had jogged faithfully around the Rockefeller every morning, and was sure to out-ski the best of his colleagues at every Aspen meeting he attended. But his heart was pounding well over a hundred, his legs shaky. He could barely keep himself up, much less carry a man, and fifty years worth of documents, an indeterminate number of miles down a tunnel that seemed more mythical than real.

Boris was scared, too. No one had ever really used the exit tunnel. He had a premonition about the back-door exit since he had arrived. "It's a haunted tunnel. If I go through there, I will die. My demons are in that place."

"Your demons are in your fucking head!!"

"But the demons. You go. I can stay. The demons will..."

Geoff was not about to take any more crap or riddles. Putting a gag around Boris' mouth was cruel, but necessary. Besides, if the old man went into seizures again, as was often the case in times of stress with advanced Scrapies, at least an airway could be kept open.

The exit down to the tunnel had a picture of Jim Morrison over the entrance. A subtle joke, Geoff thought. "Break on Through to the Other Side" came from a portable cassette player as soon as Geoff latched the door behind him. Then a timer. Counting down from ten. The music - "This is the End." Then lights illuminating hand-made sighs on the wall which read "run like hell, motherfucker," in English, German and Russian.

Geoff's feet found out just how fast they could run down an abandoned mine shaft in ten seconds. Alongside him, sheep, cattle, and human bones and, of course, rats, most of whom seem to be as brave as lions and as crazy as loons.

"Rats. Strange to be done in by rats," Geoff thought, as he saw his life ending before his eyes. It was all he remembered until the blast that shook the mud-lined escape tunnel as well as everything above it.

It felt like the California earthquake, from the INSIDE of the earth. "The End" - for every soldier who found his way into the interrogation room. And for the politicians and scientists who stood behind the barricade. "Another fuckin' 'missing' town," Geoff said. "How many 'missing' towns do you have in the goddamn country?"

Boris removed his gag. "As many as you do, or will."

The remark rang true. East and West were falling. Perhaps the only reason why Geoff hung in was to pillage what he could before the invasion of barbarians from Tokyo, Singapore, or any Latin American country that could get its networking shit together. Still, the world had to know what happened here. And what would happen out there if the secrets were lost.

"Shit. The YELLOW file," Geoff screamed. "I forgot to get the yellow file. The one with names on them. The list of the bad guys"

"Take care of the good guys first," Boris said. "More important to save the living than to get revenge on the wicked. God gets revenge on the wicked better than we do. But we are better at being merciful to victims than God is. I can't understand it, but I think it's like that."

A moment of reflection. It was unprofessional for a doctor to verbalize his thinking before it was packaged as a diagnosis. But Geoff had become a very unprofessional thinker over the last 8 hours. "I have to go back. The rest of the files might be..."

A creak of the roof, then a siren. Then, in the tunnel, approaching fast from behind on the railroad track towards

Geoff and Boris, one car, creaking down with a steady rhythm.

"The messenger of death. He's come for me," Boris said. "Time for you to got back to the land of the living. More painful than the world of the dead, but more wondrous."

"We're getting out of here together. Shut the fuck up!"

Geoff ran. "A quarter of a mile more to the exit 'door'," he said, as he looked hopefully at the maps Yakov left carved on the walls. "A quarter of a fuckin' mile more."

There was a mile worth of "quarter mile" signs. At least that's how it seemed. The faster Geoff ran, the faster the unheard pursuer followed. Always keeping a distance. A constant distance. "Elvis," Geoff said. "Maybe Elvis has been hiding out in Russia. He's designed this whole thing like an amusement ride. The secrets. The stories. The rats. This whole experience since New York has been a warped Elvis trick."

Why Geoff broke into "My Way," in that bold, deep voice that he ridiculed so much in public, but liked in private, he couldn't say. But it was good enough for Boris to join in.

"My Way" echoed against the walls for four choruses. Then Geoff improvised one. Boris improvised the next. The run turned into a bold walk. Boris regained enough strength to walk with Geoff. "Better to walk to your end than to be carried there," he said.

Their voices rose. The fates rewarded them. At the end of the tunnel - light. Sunlight seemed to shine down especially for them.

Like good old times, Boris had with the Major, Geoff thought. But this moment was about feeling, not thinking. Nothing could defeat the duo now. Nothing.

Nothing except the inevitable. And a slick of grease.

A sprained ankle for Geoff. A broken back for Boris. The kind that comes in with the gravest prognosis, even before the first X-ray is taken. Voluntary movement below the neck, gone. The touch in the fingers, gone. Deep pain sensation, gone.

"I knew it would come like this, the end," Boris said, looking at the body that had served him so well for nearly a century. "And the beginning," he continued. He looked at the light coming through the tunnel exit.

In an underground clearing leading to a ramp connected to what seemed to be an unlocked door, a VW bus appeared., With a personalized license plate reading

"ALIVE." On the windshield, a rabbit. He that said 'hello' with his nose, then hopped back towards the surface, opening the door just enough to reveal a sunlit sky behind it.

"Your chauffeur," Boris said.

The last chorus belonged to Boris. He sang it alone. He wanted it that way. Then, with a twinkle in his eye and a clenched fist, it was time. "It was not so easy a ride. But I beat the demon. I beat the demon."

With that, life left Boris' body. Fast, quicker than Geoff had seen anyone else die before.

Coming up from behind, the demon. An old mining car, driven by an automatic engine. It was an old Soviet invention, intended to seek out voices and find people. People who were needed to be found or executed. It stopped in front of Boris. Why was yet another question on a long list that would be answered someday - maybe.

Geoff never cried for anyone. Even himself. It was now time for the floodgates to open. "Damn you, old man. Damn you, you sadistic bastard." Geoff screamed, tears flowing down his face. "You make me feel pain, then give me no way to deal with it. I've protected myself from pain for a lifetime, and now you gave me enough to last three lifetimes. And no happiness to go with it. Why the hell did you give me the ability to feel pain, but not enjoy happiness?"

It was a Ukrainian curse and blessing. But Geoff was grateful to be alive, even if it cost him a lifetime of comfort. He could never be comfortable again, no matter what he did.

To die in a tunnel like this was not the kind of death life should have granted Boris. Geoff, not content to accept life's terms, intervened.

Next to the exit door, axes. Sharp enough to do the job. The last coincidence. The last time he would be this protected by the Spirits. He did the only honorable and necessary thing.

CHAPTER 14

The exit out of Leningrad was as uneventful as the flight in, at least from the customs perspective. The formalin jar containing a human brain had no problem getting through customs, even with a skull and eyes attached to it.

"I'm shipping the rest of the body back with the dope in the next shipment," Geoff thought under his breath, as a baffled customs inspector wondered why a man with so many professional degrees seemed so desperate to go home.

"Pass," the agent said after a surprisingly not too tense delay. "Have a nice trip."

It was all that was said. All the other papers and body parts from Boris that weren't left behind for the rats went through customs with no problem. So easy, Geoff thought ominously. Maybe Yakov had prearranged this, too. Maybe it was because the Soviet Union would fall any day now, and this customs official just wanted to go home, wherever that was. Was it a coincidence that Boris's death happened on the same day the Soviet Politburo dissolved itself? Could one small man in low places move so many in higher positions? Could one person make so much difference?

Boris used the Spirits a lot, Geoff thought, as he sat down in the first-class lounge on the Trans Atlantic jet that would take him home. Provided for reading material, USA Today and Pravda. Both seemed very much alike. The same lies. The same assurances to a troubled world that all is okay. Streisand playing Red Square. Plans for the first American-Russian joint sitcom, to be shot in Toronto.

Geoff smiled, then went to sleep. Maybe it was all a bad dream. He was awakened somewhere over the English Channel by Flight Attendant Oksana Strevotsky. Russian fire and an L.A. body that could open the eyes of a blind man.

"Doctor Weinburg," she said.

"Geoff."

"Your meal. Mutton. Lightly cooked. The last one, I'm afraid."

"Lamb. With basil and garlic." A sense of resolve swept through him.

"Excuse me, is something wrong?" She was genuinely concerned. Something beyond her professional job description.

Much work was ahead for Geoff. Not enough to discuss with a friend he just met. She looked over at the pile of papers next to him.

"Could you put those in the overhead compartment. Airline rules. Or I can..."

She reached down to take the papers. Geoff held them close.

"Naw. I need them. Very important project."

"Which is?" she asked in a tone more friendly than vicious.

"I'm opening a chain of vegetarian restaurants back home."

ABOUT THE AUTHOR

MJ Politis departed the womb in Hoboken, New Jersey, in 1951. To make good on what everyone who supported, taught and challenged him did, he obtained a Ph.D. in physiology in 1978 which was used to publish 46 research papers in medical journals in reconstructive neurology, toxicology and cancer treatment. He went on to obtain a veterinary degree to extend medical care to fur bearing souls in a wide variety of clinics and cultural settings across the US and Canada. In order to diagnose and cure numerous maladies of the human soul, he obtained an H.B.A.R.P. degree (human being, aspiring Renaissance person) as author of over 80 novels and novellas, as well as producer/director/writer on 27 comedo-dramatic films, which can be accessed through www.longriderpress.net. He has been owned by horses for the last 40 years, currently residing in Interior British Columbia, Canada as home base, regularly commuting to New York to maintain global perspective.